The Politics of Murder

A Thriller by

Nick Pignatelli

This is a work of fiction. Names, characters, places, and incidents either are the products of the author's imagination or are used fictitiously. Any resemblance to actual events, locales, organizations, business establishments, or persons, living or dead, is entirely coincidental and beyond the intent of the author.

THE POLITICS OF MURDER

ISBN: 1523982950
ISBN-13: 978-1523982950

Cover design by Maria Sohn

Photograph of Nick Pignatelli by Joyce Pignatelli

www.nickpignatelli.com

Facebook: Author, Nick Pignatelli

PRAISE FOR *The Devil's Claw*

The Devil's Claw is a striking first effort by Nick Pignatelli.
-- Edward Peck, author of the novel, *Lincoln's Secret.*

Pignatelli's nonstop action and clever plot twists kept me turning pages.
-- Stephen Gannon, Amazon bestselling author of The Kane Novel Series.

Nick Pignatelli's debut thriller, *The Devil's Claw*, is a page-turner reminiscent of Clive Cussler's best.
-- Robert Knightly, author of the novels, *Bodies In Winter* and *The Cold Room*.

The Devil's Claw will appeal to fans of Tom Clancy, Larry Bond, and Joseph Heller.
-- Penn Book Review.

DEDICATION

To Joyce, my wife and best friend, for your endless love and belief in me over the decades.

I can't remember a time when you were not in my life, cheering me on, and brightening every day.

* * *

"When the morning sun comes pouring through my window,

And settles on you sleeping so softly.

I know in my heart, you are the one for me.

You're all the things I've dreamed of come true."

And I Love You (Just A Little More)

Music and lyrics by Nick Pignatelli

Chapter One
Albany, NY
April 17th, 11:27 PM

Cold rain plummeted from a dark, angry sky. Thunder rumbled through the clouds and sporadic spears of white-hot lightning ripped the night wide open. And there was blood. So much blood.

My finger stabbed at the radio button. "Shots fired! Officer down!"

"Say again."

"This is Officer Rick Patterson. My partner's been shot. We're in the alley behind Four Balls Pawn Shop."

I heard the call go out for other officers in the area to converge on our location.

Huddled on the wet pavement of a dark alley near the NYS Capitol, I cradled my partner, Sergeant Dave Taylor, pleading with him not to die, believing my prayers might actually stop the inevitable.

The wail of distant sirens grew louder. "Dave, it's Rick. Help's almost here. Hang on."

The steady rain cascaded down my face, washing my tears away but not my growing heartache. Dave Taylor's brown eyes stared into the moisture-laden blackness above the alley. His breathing was labored. I tried to shield my partner's face from the heavy rain. No matter how hard I jammed my handkerchief against the ragged red hole in his chest, the blood kept flowing. Lightning lit the alley for a fraction of a second.

"Look at me, Dave," I said. His eyelids fluttered. "Stay with me."

Thunder crashed down around my wounded partner and me. Blue-uniformed figures burst into the narrow passage, weapons drawn, heavy boots pounding through the dirty rainwater. Flashlight beams left red circles in my eyes. The officers shouted too many questions. I tightened my grip on Dave. "The shooter ran down the alley," I said. They took off at a dead run, illumination from their flashlights bouncing wildly off the wet ground before fading into the night.

A paramedic dropped to his knees next to us. He tugged on my arm, trying to get me to release my grip on Dave. "You gotta let him go so I can help him," he said. I reluctantly let Dave go and staggered to my feet. I stood in silence and watched as a second paramedic worked feverishly to save my partner.

"Patterson!" Someone shook me, shouted in my ear. Tearing my eyes from Dave, I found myself staring at our lieutenant, Larry Dawson. "Damnit, Rick! What the hell happened?"

I tried to focus. As I wiped rain from my face, I froze at the sight of my handkerchief. The white material was soaked with Dave's blood.

"We answered a call. Dave told me to wait while he flushed the perp out. I told him to let me go in first, but he said no." The paramedic bore down on Dave's chest. "I went anyway and Dave turned to grab me. That's when he got shot."

A police officer emerged from the darkness at the far end of the alley. “The shooter’s gone.”

Lieutenant Dawson put his hand on my shoulder and leaned in. Rain spilled from the brim of his cap. “Rick, did you get a look at the shooter?” Two paramedics loaded Dave on a gurney; he wasn’t moving. “Officer Patterson, did you see him?”

“No.”

Paramedics hustled Dave to the ambulance. The red lights on the vehicle’s roof threw angry, chaotic shadows all around me. I stared helplessly as the ambulance carrying the man who was my partner, my mentor, and my friend faded into the darkness.

* * *

Five years later, I stared down the length of that same alley, my trembling hands jammed into my trouser pockets. I seemed to find myself at this same spot every year on April 17th. Garbage overflowed from half-rusted trash containers. Graffiti decorated the weathered brick walls. My vision blurred. The sounds of the city at noon were all around me. There was no sign that Dave Taylor had died so violently here. Jagged shards of memories cut into my mind, the pain as real now as it had been the night Dave was robbed of his life.

At the time Dave was shot, I had been an officer on Albany's police force for two years. My downward spiral began with a pistol's muzzle flash followed by the loud crack of a deadly bullet racing toward me. Fate intervened and that bullet stopped short. My partner, Dave Taylor, took a slug with my name on it. It was all over in a fraction of a second. The police academy had given me the best training they could, but they never taught me how to deal with the loss of my partner.

Sergeant Dave Taylor was one of the most revered members of Albany's police force. He was considered by many to be a cornerstone of the force. Dave had been around for decades and trained countless men and women. His death was a blow many of the other officers had trouble absorbing. A blow many blamed on me.

An exhaustive investigation cleared me of any wrongdoing but it was not enough to quell the damage to my reputation. None of the other officers wanted to partner up with the infamous Rick Patterson. After a year, I resigned from the police force. By that time, my girlfriend had walked out on me. At twenty-six, my promising career in law enforcement lay in ashes at my feet.

Not knowing what else to do, I opened a private investigation service above *Tommy G's*, a popular restaurant on Albany's North Pearl Street. Through a door at the rear of the office was a small kitchenette, full bathroom, living room, and a single bedroom. It wasn't much, but it was home for now.

In honor of my slain partner, I named my new business *Patterson & Taylor Investigative Services.* I wish I could say that being a private investigator was as exciting and lucrative as depicted by Thomas Magnum and Mike Hammer, but most months I made just enough to survive.

To make matters worse, the shooter who ended Dave Taylor's life had never been found. That was something else that haunted me, maybe another thing that kept me from moving forward.

The sound of a city bus roaring past the alley entrance at my back jarred me. It was time to go. Another year in the books.

"See you next year, partner," I said. With this year's

pilgrimage over, I squared my shoulders and strode away. I bowed my head and left the shadows of the alley behind me.

Chapter Two
Schenectady, NY
June 28, 12:03 PM

Gregory Rockwell sat alone in a tiny room at the rear of a dilapidated, no-questions-asked boarding house. Perched on the edge of a rickety chair, he glared at a small television.

Helen Clifton, well into her second term as governor of New York, spewed political rhetoric at throngs of supporters in a live broadcast. Resplendent in her trademark sky-blue business suit, she stood behind an ornate podium festooned with microphones on gooseneck stands. The NYS Capitol in Albany filled the background; brilliant sunshine beamed down upon her.

Clifton's formal announcement regarding her entrance into the upcoming presidential election was scheduled for July 4th at a gala event still in the planning stages. People in the know mentioned the deck of the renovated USS *Slater* museum in downtown Albany as the perfect location.

Major polls showed Clifton peaking at the right moment for her big move to the oval office. Talking heads agreed it was her time.

Gregory Rockwell also agreed it was her time, but not to rise to the highest office in the land. He slipped a faded, dog-eared photograph from his shirt pocket. His calloused fingers held it as if it were a delicate piece of parchment. A young couple kneeled on a well-manicured lawn, a young boy held a tiny dog between them; a palatial mansion stood in the background.

Rockwell closed his eyes, his mind tuning out Clifton's latest campaign promises, his thoughts drifting back in time. He could almost smell the newly mown grass in the photograph, the warm sun on his face, his Yorkshire Terrier snuggled in his arms.

His grandfather, Joseph Rockwell, built a thriving shipping empire from nothing. His father, Thomas Rockwell, eventually took over and expanded the family business to include a new wave of computer technology the maritime industry had been reluctant to embrace. At the top of his game, the political bug bit Thomas Rockwell; he decided the time was right for a successful businessman to grab the reins of governmental power.

Thomas Rockwell was a smart, honest man, but he had no idea what was in store when he entered the political arena for the New York governorship against Helen Clifton. Clifton's political party saw her as a rising star; the people pulling the strings had big plans for her future and vowed to let nothing stand in their way.

Rockwell's popularity soared in early polls but crashed once Clifton's election machine took every innocent event in Rockwell's life and dragged it through the mud. His most loyal supporters and business associates backed away. His dive in the polls picked up speed. The architects of Clifton's campaign smelled blood and kicked their efforts into overdrive.

When the campaign ended, Helen Clifton was a shiny, new governor on the verge of a brilliant career in politics and Thomas Rockwell was a broken man. It was a classic example of being politically mugged. Rockwell's time and money were wasted in a fruitless effort to defend his character instead of addressing issues. The nonstop onslaught of negative accusations and falsehoods from the Clifton campaign had all but destroyed Rockwell's reputation and that of his business empire. He dumped his holdings for what little he could get and withdrew from the public eye.

Gregory Rockwell was in his junior year of college at Rensselaer Polytechnic Institute pursuing a degree in electrical engineering when the Rockwell dream crashed and burned. Suzanne Rockwell took the easy way out—in a drunken stupor, she drove her car into a tree. His beloved wife's death plunged Thomas Rockwell into a nervous breakdown that left him in a catatonic trance. The former giant of industry spent his final days staring blankly at the cracks in the ceiling above his hospital bed.

Before the bottom completely fell out, Thomas Rockwell had managed to stash away a trust fund for his only child. It was the only thing that survived the mind-boggling demise of the Rockwell fortune.

With his family gone, Gregory Rockwell left the shattered remnants of his old life behind. He wandered the country trying to forget his past and searching for a future. While he had been a handsome, athletic young man, Rockwell now sported shaggy hair, an unshaven face, wore thrift shop clothing, and lived out of a tattered backpack he scavenged from a Dumpster. He walked, hitchhiked, and rode buses. He worked menial short-term jobs and dealt only in cash.

Years of aimless drifting found Gregory Rockwell on

the side of a dusty road somewhere in the Southwest. He sat on his backpack under a sweltering sun, a week-old newspaper found along the road clutched in his hand. Rockwell stared at an article on the front page that mentioned Helen Clifton as a shoe-in for the next President of the United States. He couldn't help but think that could have been his father. *Should* have been. He pondered the only future that finally made sense—Clifton had ruined his life, he would return the favor.

Rockwell stood, hurled the newspaper to the ground, and defiantly thrust his thumb out at an approaching pickup truck well beyond its prime. The battered vehicle rattled to a stop amidst a cloud of dust and blue-gray exhaust. Rockwell threw his backpack into the cargo bed and slid onto the cracked vinyl bench seat. He finally had somewhere to be.

A blast of sound from the television brought Rockwell back to the present. Helen Clifton stood beaming, the deafening cheers from her adoring supporters washing over her.

She had stolen everything from him. Now she would pay. Rockwell jammed the photo back into his shirt pocket. He pointed at Clifton's image on the screen, index finger extended, middle, ring, and little fingers curled, thumb angled toward the ceiling; his hand resembled a pistol. "Enjoy yourself, Madame Governor. Your reign is about to come to a tragic end."

Chapter Three
Staten Island, NY
June 28, 8:12 PM

Darkness settled over Staten Island as Carter Anson swung his weathered black Ford pickup off Richmond Terrace and passed through the East Yard entrance of Caddell Dry Dock & Repair Company. He maneuvered his truck into the small employee parking area and ground to a halt.

Anson killed the headlights and engine, then spent a moment gathering his thoughts. And his resolve. He had agreed to this fool's errand but now doubt seeped into his mind. He grabbed a balled-up blue bandana from the passenger seat and mopped the perspiration from his forehead. Could he actually go through with this? It was a simple enough task and the payoff would be huge. His fingers tapped the steering wheel.

Carter Anson didn't really know anything about the guy who hired him, just that he offered him an obscene amount of money to smuggle something aboard an old warship in dry dock for repairs. In the end he knew he had to do the deed because in his world it always came down to money. And the 51-year-old Anson was in desperate need. A serious drinker with a bad gambling problem and three ex-wives, he was willing to lay it all on this one last bet that could get him clear. Or thrown in prison. Either way his troubles would be over.

The USS *Slater* (DE766) was the last World War II destroyer escort afloat in America. Originally launched in 1944, it now served as a floating museum moored near the Capitol in Albany. The vintage warship was currently in Caddell Dry Dock & Repair Company undergoing long overdue hull repairs. Soon tugboats would move the vessel back up the Hudson River to Albany where it would once again be open to the public.

A few weeks ago Carter Anson stopped at a favorite watering hole for shipyard workers and became an unwitting pawn in a plot bigger than anything he could have ever imagined. A stranger appeared at his elbow, helped himself to the stool next to Anson's, and struck up a conversation. Anson had never noticed the guy in the bar but that didn't mean he hadn't been there before. The stranger bought him a drink and as the night went on, and the drinks kept coming, Anson told him he worked at Caddell's Dry Dock as a welder. After that the stranger showed up every time Anson did. Before he knew what had happened, Carter Anson laid out his tale of economic woes. The mystery man eventually asked if Anson would be working on a specific vessel due to arrive for repairs. Anson wasn't sure but thought he probably would.

And that was the moment Gregory Rockwell sank his hook into Carter Anson and reeled him in. Rockwell had his plan to bring down Governor Helen Clifton all laid out; he needed the unsuspecting Anson to set the stage for the final showdown.

* * *

It was rumored in local newspapers that Governor Helen Clifton would be tossing her hat into the upcoming presidential campaign from the decks of the *Slater* on July 4th. Her grandfather had been a Navy man and she planned to tap into that patriotism to garner as many votes as she could. As soon as Rockwell read a follow-up article about the USS *Slater* being moved from Albany to Caddell's Dry Dock on Staten Island for repairs, a brilliant plan for the perfect act of revenge coalesced in his tortured mind. He hopped a bus from Albany to Staten Island and began to tail the workers coming to and going from Caddell's until he found one who could be lured by the promise of easy money. There's one in every bunch, and Carter Anson was that one.

Anson named the amount of cash he would need to accommodate Gregory Rockwell's mysterious request, never expecting him to go along with it. Rockwell agreed without question. One day later he delivered half the cash to Anson along with three rucksacks, the balance to be paid as soon as the *Slater* returned to the Port of Albany. Anson was to stash the rucksacks in three spots shown on a schematic of the hull spaces downloaded from the *Slater*'s website. Rockwell gave him one warning—do not open the rucksacks, no matter what. If he did, all bets were off. Blinded by dollar signs, Anson agreed.

Any doubts Carter Anson initially had evaporated when he opened the small duffel bag Rockwell handed him in the bar's darkened parking lot. It was stuffed with cash, almost to the point of overflowing. Anson couldn't fathom how this scruffy-looking young guy had actually come up with this much money. It briefly crossed his mind he might be the target of an undercover sting. He figured if he was he'd get a low-life lawyer, scream entrapment, and cash in with a big, fat lawsuit. Somehow, some way, he was going to get paid and he didn't much care by who.

* * *

Anson 's shaking hand opened the door. He stepped out of his vehicle and looked around; he was alone in the parking area. He reached behind the driver's seat and pulled out the third and final black rucksack. The other two had been hidden aboard earlier.

Anson jammed a scarred yellow hard hat on his head, then shouldered the rucksack. He traversed the East Yard, threading his way between the string of small buildings until he came to Pier C, then followed it all the way to Dry Dock Number 6. His eyes swept left and right as he approached his destination, scanning for any workers who might still be around.

The only sound in the shipyard came from the traffic out on Richmond Terrace and the nonstop jet airliners traversing the skies over New York City. After one more look to verify he was alone, he climbed the weather-beaten scaffold alongside the huge ship sitting on blocks in Dry Dock Number 6. Flakes of mustard-colored paint fell from the handrails as he made his way up the aged scaffold.

At the top of the twenty-six-foot-high scaffold, Anson clambered aboard the main deck of the *Slater*, just forward of the starboard K-gun depth charge racks. He carefully lowered the heavy rucksack to the deck. He was confident he was all alone on the vessel.

After tonight, Anson's part of the operation would be complete. With any luck it would never be traced back to him, but just in case he had already put together his own plan to disappear. As soon as the warship docked in Albany he would get the rest of his money. And vanish in a way that could make the Great Houdini jealous.

Carter Anson shouldered the rucksack, ducked through an open hatch and disappeared down the dark corridor leading to the bowels of the old warship.

Chapter Four
Albany, NY
June 29, 12:49 PM

I leaned back against the edge of the scarred mahogany bar, a half-finished roast beef sandwich on a plate behind me, a bottle of beer in my hand. The band announced it would take a short break before returning with a set of Beatles songs. It was a full house for lunch at *Tommy G's* on North Pearl Street, the most popular eatery in downtown Albany, spitting distance from a state Capitol overflowing with fast-talking politicians and downstairs from my combination office/apartment.

A heavy hand slapped the counter behind me. I spun around to see Tommy Griesau, the owner, a bar rag over his shoulder and stern look on his face. "You here to take in the scenery or spend some damn money?" A wide grin split Griesau's face. "How the hell are you, Rick Patterson, you mangy old sonofabitch?"

"Never better, Tommy G," I said. "Looks like a pretty good crowd."

"Yeah, adding a live band during lunch was a stroke of genius on my part."

"So my suggestion that live music at lunchtime might bring in more business had nothing to do with your stroke of genius?"

Griesau looked up at the pressed tin ceiling. "I don't know, Rick. I don't seem to recall that conversation."

"You're killing me, Tommy." Griesau cracked up and I couldn't help but join in. Tommy Griesau was good people, pure and simple.

"So what's new, Rick? How's business?"

"Same old crap. Make a buck, lose two."

"I thought you were gonna pick up some security work when the governor gives her big speech on July 4th?"

"Think I had a shot until my paperwork ended up on my old lieutenant's desk. As soon as Dawson saw my name, I was dead in the water."

"Jesus, Rick, you were cleared of that shooting thing a long time ago. I can't believe they're still holding that over you."

I took a long pull from my bottle of beer. "Yeah, well, believe it."

A voice interrupted our conversation. "Well, now, do my eyes deceive me or is that Rick Patterson, Albany's superhero private investigator?"

Tommy Griesau and I turned our heads to see two Albany Police Department officers with whom I had started my career. They were still on the force. And I was not. Their usual ball-busting was about to begin. Tipping my bottle at them, I nodded, then turned back to Griesau.

The taller of the two was a rugged man with blond hair named Steve Flynn; his companion, Dave Witkowski, was short with a swarthy complexion and slick, black hair. Both were out of uniform. "What's the matter, Ricky?" said Flynn. "Aren't you happy to see your old police buddies?"

I refused to acknowledge Flynn and Witkowski. I rubbed my thumb up and down the condensation-soaked label on my beer. Griesau looked on in silence. "I used to be on the force with these two," I explained.

"Probably pondering his next big case or thinking about working with his good old police pals on the governor's security detail," Witkowski said.

Flynn faked a deep-in-thought look. "I heard he was turned down for the security detail. Again."

Slamming my bottle on the bar, I glared at the two men. They grinned like a pair of idiots. I felt Griesau's hand on my arm.

"I don't care if you two are cops. I suggest you move on. Now."

"Hey, pal. All we want is something to eat," Flynn said.

"You might want to try someplace on Lark Street. Maybe you can find a place that caters to assholes."

"Watch what you say," Flynn cautioned. "I'm sure you'll need us before we need you. And when you do, maybe we'll be a little late getting here."

"Maybe you should watch what you say," said Griesau. "One call to my uncle at city hall and I guarantee you two will be servicing parking meters for the rest of your illustrious police careers."

"Let it go, Tommy," I said.

"My house, my rules." Griesau waved Flynn and Witkowski toward the door. "There it is, boys. Don't let it hit you in the ass on the way out."

Flynn shoved Witkowski's shoulder. "C'mon. I heard the food here is crap anyway."

"You'll never find out," Griesau said. "And don't ever come back."

"I never knew you had an uncle on the force," I said.

"I don't. All you gotta do is mention city hall and the rats always scatter."

I pulled some cash from my pocket. "Gotta run, Tommy. I'm hoping to scare up some business out on the mean streets of the big city."

"Not today, Ricky. It's on the house."

"No kidding?"

"You bet. Throwing those two punk-ass cops outta here was the most fun I've had all week." He whipped the soiled bar cloth from his shoulder and wiped down the counter. I stuffed the cash back in my pocket. Maybe this was going to be a good day after all.

As soon as I stepped out into the warm, spring sunshine, my cell phone chirped. *One missed call.* I took a deep breath hoping it wasn't another bill collector, then pressed the symbol to retrieve the voicemail message.

I had no idea just how much that seemingly inconsequential action would turn my whole life upside down. As the message played, I recognized the caller's voice immediately, a voice belonging to someone who had left my life years ago.

"Uh, hi, Rick. This is Kyle." A deep breath. "Kyle Fitzpatrick. I know it's been a while, but I need your help." Silence for a second. "It's a matter of life and death." I stared at the phone's screen, hardly believing I had just gotten a call from the older brother of Megan Fitzpatrick, my former girlfriend. I hadn't spoken to Kyle or Megan since she walked out on me four years ago. I jabbed the keypad with a reluctant finger.

Chapter Five
Troy, NY
June 29, 11:34 PM

The three men huddled around a makeshift table, faces illuminated by weak flashlights. Tonight they met in Troy in an abandoned apartment building in a seedy neighborhood. It was a location on their list of random gathering sites scattered around the Capital Region of New York.

Whispering conspiratorially, they went through the details of their plan. One called it necessary to put the country back on the right track. The rest voiced agreement. A different voice expressed concern about time growing short and much still to do. Then they all laughed about what they would do with their payoffs.

An up-and-coming political faction had taken root in America. The group's supporters were scattered around the country, their numbers growing, but not fast enough to have an impact on the looming presidential election. Speculation had tagged the current governor of New York, Helen Clifton, as the next president. The rumored successor to the throne would never support their agenda. The three men in the room had one mission: cause chaos that would blow back on the New York governor and her administration, and derail her ascension to the White House. At least that was their cover story.

In the beginning, Gregory Rockwell, their leader, and his two associates spent an entire year trolling the endless throngs marching around Albany's Capitol building on an almost daily basis either protesting against, or rallying for, something. They circled the crowds, darting in and out, like sharks hunting for prey. In time, they found plenty of recruits who were happy to fill their ranks, but none were allowed in the inner circle. The newbies were simply camouflage.

Rockwell sported a confident smile. "Clifton will speak at the College for Nanoscale Science and Engineering in three days. We need to flood the place with anti-Clifton signs and angry constituents. That place is one of the jewels in her crown. We have to steal it from her."

"Is it smoke time?" asked Phil Crowley, one of Rockwell's associates. Crowley was referring to their plan to use non-lethal smoke bombs to disrupt and disperse any attendees not persuaded by negative signs and chants denouncing Helen Clifton and her policies.

"Not yet, but we're getting close," said Rockwell. "And we're still on track for the big day."

Crowley and Tony Zacarelli, another associate, murmured. It was shaping up to be a July 4th that would long be remembered.

With their plans set for Clifton's next appearance, Gregory Rockwell sent them on their way. He turned off the remaining flashlight, moved to a cracked window, and stared through the grimy glass as Crowley and Zacarelli hit the street. Gregory Rockwell swelled with assurance.

He had made the perfect decision in choosing them.

Rockwell's grand scheme began in America's Southwest when he found a group of protesters who supported his hatred of Helen Clifton and her plans to ascend to the White House. He wormed his way into the ruling faction, persuading them to let him head up the group that would haunt Clifton's every move in New York State. Once he convinced them of his loyalty, he covertly assembled his own group, people not driven by ideology but by material wealth. In Oklahoma, he found Phil Crowley, a smart but short-tempered thug with a real talent for electronics and explosives. In Kentucky, he recruited Tony Zacarelli, a petty thief and fast talker. Neither gave a damn about politics, but they loved money, the more the better, and that is how Gregory Rockwell secured their loyalty. With their help, Rockwell would use his father's money to exact revenge against Clifton and destroy her. It was the perfect way to settle the score for the way she destroyed his life. And his entire family's.

My guys are still charged up from their escapade this morning involving the girl, thought Rockwell. *I was careless and it almost cost us everything.* He shook his head. Too bad he might have to sacrifice her for his plan to come to fruition. He left the building and disappeared into the darkness. Rockwell had one loose end to worry about, her fate still undecided.

Chapter Six
Albany, NY
June 30, 6:03 AM

I sat alone in a popular coffee shop on the northern end of Albany's Wolf Road. Absently swirling the remains of black coffee in my cup, I squinted into the early morning sun flooding through the window. An endless caravan of vehicles sped up and down the busy road.

Kyle Fitzpatrick had not said what his problem was when we spoke over the phone, just that he needed my help. *Life and death* was the phrase he used again. I had reluctantly agreed to meet him the next morning. Four years since I had seen or heard from Megan or her brother and now this, whatever this was.

A squeaky hinge on the front door drew my attention. Kyle Fitzpatrick stepped through the doorway; his eyes darted around the room, then settled on me. He strode across the checkerboard tile floor toward my booth, dropped onto the orange vinyl bench, and slid to a stop across from me.

I shrugged. "Well?"

"I'm not sure where to start." Kyle scoped out the

early morning customers. "I can't believe what I've gotten myself into," he whispered.

"Kyle, why are we here? What's going on?"

"It's Megan."

I was fully focused after hearing my ex-girlfriend's name. "Is Megan okay?"

"Yes...no." Kyle raked his fingers through his thick black hair. "I don't really know."

Kyle wiped his sweaty palms on his shirt. "You remember I was always trying to get a gig reporting for a newspaper, television station, whatever, right?" He shifted his weight. "Well, Megan told me she was approached by some people at a rally at the Capitol. Said they were trying to recruit her for some protest group. She got the impression they might be on the radical side, maybe willing to use violence to achieve their goals. She thought there might be a story there. I told her to play along and then bring me in." He paused. "Rick, I swear, I was just trying to get a good story. If these people turned out to be major players I thought I could maybe snag a real reporting job."

"So where's Megan?" I tried to swallow my impatience.

"I don't know. Someone snatched her."

"Are you telling me Megan was kidnapped?" My voice rose causing heads to turn.

Kyle held up his hand to quiet me down. "Please, whoever grabbed her could be following me. She's being held but I don't know where. A guy called me from her cell phone yesterday, said he knew who I was and what I was planning to do. He said if I told anyone about him or that he's holding her I'll never see her again. Then he promised that if I went silent she'd be released unharmed on July 4th. Even told me where I would find her and what time. Then he cut the connection."

I tried to work things out in my head. "Have you contacted the authorities?"

"I can't. He said he has eyes in the Albany Police Department."

"And you believe him?"

"I don't know. Do I gamble with Megan in his hands?"

A maelstrom of thoughts and emotions whirled inside my head. "Why?" I said.

Kyle looked confused. "Why what?"

"Why me?"

"Look, Rick. No matter what you think, Megan never stopped caring about you, even when things fell apart. She was never serious about anybody after you two—"

"—went our separate ways," I cut in. I knew our breakup had been my fault. I had been impossible to live with after Dave Taylor was killed. I spoke softly. "And I never stopped caring about Megan." This was the first time I had ever admitted it, the first time out loud anyway.

"I think she always hoped you guys would get back together." Kyle leaned forward. "Please, Rick. I can't trust anyone with Megan's life but you."

My eyes settled on the bustling traffic just outside the window. There had been many times when I wanted to reach out to Megan and probably should have. But I was a man whose pride surrounded me like an impenetrable wall, and I had never been quite able to break through. Maybe if I had one more chance.

Now I wondered if Kyle was paranoid or if his fears were legitimate. "Okay, Kyle. Let's go over this, top to bottom. And don't leave anything out."

Kyle cracked a thin smile. "This is gonna make one helluva story, Rick."

My grim glare wiped the smile off Kyle's face. "This is about getting Megan back safe, not some story to help your career. And one more thing—if I say we're in over our heads, we bring in help."

"But he said he had people inside the APD—"

"There's a local FBI office on McCarty Avenue in Albany that we can turn to if need be. And two agents there I would trust with my life."

"Okay. You call the shots. One hundred percent."

"One hundred percent, Kyle. Don't forget it."

Kyle absently toyed with a packet of sugar.

"Kyle. Focus, okay?"

He tossed the sugar packet onto the table. "Sorry, Rick. Just wondering if I'm ever going to see my little sister again."

"We're going to get Megan back," I said. "I give you my word." A thought suddenly came to me. "What about Megan not showing up for work? Won't someone start asking questions?"

"Before the guy cut the connection he told me to call Megan's office and tell them she would be out of town until after the 4th of July. To blame it on a non-fatal family emergency. I called her supervisor. He said Megan had so much vacation time built up she deserved to be out for a while."

It sounded like the guy who had snatched Megan Fitzpatrick knew exactly what he was doing. Had he done this before? If so, I might be going up against a pro. And was he working alone or with a crew? These were the unknowns that might change the rules of the game.

"What do you know about the group Megan was talking about?"

"Not a lot. I met the guy who said he was running the show. Young guy. Said his name was Gregory but wouldn't give his last name."

"Did this Gregory guy mention anyone else?"

"No. I think he was ready to bring me into the group but that's when my cover got blown. I think he may be the guy who called me on her phone." Kyle's shoulders sagged. "It was just stupid, bad timing. And Megan paid the price."

"Nobody paid anything yet." I pulled a small notepad and pen from my back pocket and flipped it open to a blank page. "I need you to describe this guy. And give me as much detail as you can."

"Like I said, he was a young guy. Late twenties, early thirties. Not bad looking. Shaggy brown hair. Hazel eyes. No real beard or moustache. Just a couple days of growth. I put him around six feet, give or take an inch or two. Somewhere around 190 to 210 pounds. Not muscular but fit. Always wore a black hoodie, faded jeans. Dark sunglasses, too. Aviator style."

"Any idea why they're willing to release Megan on July 4th?"

"None."

Kyle and I spent the next two hours throwing ideas and theories back and forth. We piled into my green Jeep Wrangler and left for Albany's West Capitol Park. I hoped to spot Gregory with no last name there, in the midst of today's demonstration. If we could get our hands on him I felt sure Megan would be back home by the end of the day.

I refused to consider the possibility I might not get Megan back safe. It was never far from my mind that I had failed Dave Taylor and cost my partner his life. The fact that I had been cleared did little to keep my guilt from tearing me apart. I would not fail Megan Fitzpatrick. I would give my own life before I lost hers. Guaranteed. I pressed down harder on the gas pedal, my mind racing through a thousand different scenarios, few of them good.

Chapter Seven
Albany, NY
June 30, 9:48 AM

"I don't give a damn about your issues!" New York Governor and soon-to-be presidential candidate Helen Clifton's fist slammed on her desk setting off a miniature earthquake. A silver-framed photograph of her family was the first victim; it toppled over face down. "Why are these bastards still disrupting every single event?" Her face was scarlet. She had spent her entire life getting results through screaming and intimidation, but never in the public eye. "They are too well-organized and somebody, somewhere knows something about them."

Andy Kohler, Clifton's press secretary, tried to speak. "Ma'am, please, if you'll just let me say—"

Clifton cut him off with a savage wave of her hand. "Can you hear that? They're outside right now screaming like goddamn demons! The only thing I want to hear you say is that they will not be an issue any more. You get somebody inside that damn bunch of malcontents and I mean right now." She uprighted the photograph. "I swear, if these bastards embarrass me when I make my presidential campaign announcement, you won't be able to get a job picking up dog shit in the park."

* * *

Enid Walker, Clifton's administrative assistant, sat at her desk just outside the governor's office. The attractive young woman could hear Clifton's muffled voice through the heavy wood door, then silence. Kohler quickly backed through the doorway. He leaned his portly frame against the closed door, face tilted toward the ceiling, eyes shut.

"That bad, huh?"

"Yelling, screaming, threats. So, no. No worse than usual." Kohler pulled a handkerchief from his pocket and mopped the sweat from his brow. He forced himself to breathe slowly.

"Andy, I really don't understand why you put up with her," said Walker.

Kohler put a finger to his lips and shook his head. Walker shrugged and returned to her memo. The pale, middle-aged Kohler straightened his tie, tugged on his snug sport coat, and left the office without another word. He was on a mission—to find out who was behind the protests and put a stop to them. And fast.

Andy Kohler had received confirmation that very morning that the President of the United States would be endorsing Governor Helen Clifton on the 4th of July when she announced her bid for the presidency. If anyone interfered with Clifton's big moment on the world stage, there was no doubt that he would be the first one sacrificed to the lions. And those damn lions were always hungry.

* * *

Helen Clifton paced back and forth across her huge office. She covered her ears, trying without success to shut out the sound of protestors yelling outside her window. She came to a stop before a wall covered in pictures, every one of them featuring her in the middle of the shot. The photographs formed a timeline depicting her rise to power: her days on the high school debate team; her early years as an attorney; and finally, her hard-fought political positions. She intended to add one more picture to that collection—Helen Clifton as the first female president of the United States. And God help anyone who stood in her way.

Helen Clifton's climb to power was well-documented, beginning in prep school, where she proved to be a fierce member of the debate team. It was widely known that if you went up against her on any issue, you would not only be defeated, but she would ensure you never did it again.

Clifton built upon those same tactics when she entered the field of law, further sharpening her skills and rising to new heights. From there it was a natural progression to jump into the political arena. With her husband Jeff at her side, she climbed over the bodies of her political enemies, no matter how high the piles got. It seemed she could not be stopped on her way to the presidency.

The cacophony outside intruded on her stroll down memory lane, bringing her back to the here and now. Andy Kohler. She should have dumped the old fool years ago. The problem was the media liked him. He gave a cheerful demeanor to her office. Add to that the fact that he was her husband's uncle, and it would be a political bombshell to axe him from her team. With any luck, if she kept hammering away at him, maybe he would do her a favor and drop dead from a heart attack. She already had her eyes on a new public relations person waiting in the wings, a blood-thirsty shark.

Helen Clifton spun toward the windows overlooking West Capitol Park. Her manicured hands clenched into fists. "Shut up, you bastards, or you'll all be sorry!"

Chapter Eight
Albany, NY
June 30, 12:32 PM

I sat on one of the green wooden benches lining the Washington Avenue side of Albany's West Capitol Park. Dressed in a faded blue chambray shirt and khaki slacks, I blended in with most of the lunch hour government workers cruising the park. I hid behind a pair of sunglasses, my eyes sweeping the park over the top edge of my newspaper. A brown canvas briefcase strategically placed on the bench kept anyone from sitting next to me.

It was a sunny, summer day, and yet another demonstration by unhappy citizens was taking place, providing free entertainment for the scores of government employees on their lunch breaks. My eyes tracked Kyle as he sauntered around the large park.

Food trucks and vendor carts lined the edges of the park. Kyle gave me a barely noticeable shake of his head, then stood in line at a hot dog cart. Scanning the crowd, I hoped to see someone take more than a casual interest in him. No one did. I watched Kyle place his order, pay the vendor, then walk back into the middle of the park munching on a hot dog. He moved toward a particularly loud mass of demonstrators. Standing at the edge of the group, he studied each person as they passed by chanting and waving homemade placards.

This is getting us nowhere fast. We would have to get more aggressive in our search for the person holding Megan Fitzpatrick if we hoped to find her before it was too late. July 4th was when this Gregory guy promised to let her go unharmed. But why July 4th? And even then, I feared Megan's return was not guaranteed. I shoved my emotions down. Hard. And fought to keep them down. I needed to be clear-headed and objective if I was going to find Megan Fitzpatrick in time to save her.

* * *

Phil Crowley leaned against a tree on the State Street side of the park. Rockwell had tasked him and Tony Zacarelli with keeping an eye on Kyle Fitzpatrick while Rockwell's regulars worked the crowd, stirring them up to near frenzy. Fitzpatrick's only contact had been with Gregory Rockwell. But Rockwell warned both of his top people not to be complacent just because Fitzpatrick had never met them. Rockwell had been fooled once. He would not let it happen again. There was too much at stake with only five days to go.

For more than two hours, Phil Crowley had examined Kyle Fitzpatrick's every move. A few times Fitzpatrick seemed to be looking at someone on the opposite side of the park, but the park was so crowded he had no chance of seeing who that other person might be. He hoped Tony Zacarelli, working the other side of the park, had a better view. Crowley's attention was drawn to members of his own group demonstrating in the middle of the park. A shoving match had broken out.

* * *

Andy Kohler lay flat on his back in the grass, surrounded by the people who had shoved him down. They screamed incessantly as he tried without success to get back on his feet. All he had done was approach the group and ask if he could speak with whoever was in charge. His mistake was forgetting to remove the laminated ID attached to a blue lanyard around his neck that identified him as Governor Helen Clifton's press secretary. It was like waving a red flag in front of the world's angriest bulls.

Most days there would be a police officer or two on bicycles or horseback circulating through the park. Today not a single one was in sight. Kohler found out just how true it was that there was never a cop around when you needed one.

Without warning, the crowd parted. A strong hand reached down, grabbed him by the arm, and with some effort hoisted him to his feet. Andy Kohler was not a fighter, never had been, and it was going to be evident in the next second. He jammed his eyes closed and tried to cover his face, but the hand would not release its grip.

"C'mon, move!" a voice bellowed.

Hustled away from the shaking fists and shrieking voices, Kohler was confused. The person towing him wasn't in any sort of law enforcement uniform, so who was he? When they were a safe distance from the attackers the man released Kohler's arm.

"You okay, man?" said Kyle Fitzpatrick

Kohler looked at his rescuer, then back at the attackers. He rubbed his arm, trying to get feeling back where the man's iron grip had latched onto him.

"Hey! You okay?"

"I...uh, yeah," Kohler said. "Thanks for that."

"No problem." Kyle noticed Andy Kohler's

identification badge. "What was that all about?"

"I don't know. I asked to speak to the person in charge and next thing I know I'm on the ground." Kohler brushed dirt and grass off his sport coat and dress slacks. "I just wanted to open a dialogue about their resentment toward the governor."

Kyle snuck a glance over to where Rick Patterson had been sitting; Patterson was on his feet, quickly approaching. An idea suddenly struck Kyle. He dove in head first. "You said you're looking for the guy in charge of this group?"

Kohler stopped his brushing. "Yes. I need to speak with that person and convince them to stop disrupting every rally the governor has."

Patterson was almost there, but Kyle couldn't wait. "Name's Kyle Fitzpatrick." He extended his hand.

"Andy Kohler, Governor Clifton's press secretary. You have no idea how much I appreciate you jumping in and rescuing me."

"Yeah, no problem. Here's the thing, Andy. Can I call you Andy?" Kohler nodded. "I'm an independent writer and I'm putting together a story on this group. Just like you, I'm also trying to find out who's in charge." Kyle thought there might have been a spark of interest in Kohler's eyes. "Maybe we can help each other out. You know, exchange information since we both want the same thing."

Kohler reflected on Clifton chewing him out earlier that morning and how he needed to stop the demonstrators. He needed answers fast before he was jettisoned from Clifton's inner circle. His first encounter with the group proved he had no idea what he was doing. "I think we might be able to work out an equitable arrangement."

Chapter Nine
Albany, NY
June 30, 3:02 PM

I drew up next to Kyle. "What's going on?"

"Rick Patterson, meet Andy Kohler, Governor Clifton's press secretary. Andy here is going to be working with us."

"On what?" I said.

"Andy, Rick is a private investigator working with me on this assignment." Kyle turned to me. "Andy is looking to speak with the person in charge of the demonstrators just like we are." I looked at him in silence. Kyle barreled on. "We should get out of here and exchange what we have so far."

"Give me a contact number and one hour," Kohler said. "I have to have background checks run on you both before I commit to anything. If you are who you say you are, we'll try to solve this problem together." Kohler left Kyle and me standing under one of the large shade trees dotting the park and rushed off toward his office.

One hour later, Andy Kohler had the information he needed—Kyle and I were summoned to his office.

Chapter Ten
Albany, NY
June 30, 4:37 PM

Kohler sat behind his large wooden desk; Kyle and I sat across from him. The time he chose for this meeting would keep the staff from inquiring about his late-day visitors. Kohler listened intently as we divulged what we knew of the rebellious group causing his boss, the governor, such pains. I didn't tell him we really didn't have much. At this point I was winging it.

I decided it would be best to hold back on the situation regarding Megan. "That's all we know since today was our first day trying to track down this Gregory guy. It would help if we had a last name, but we don't. The only thing we have going for us is that Kyle actually met with him and can ID him."

"But tomorrow we'll be here again," said Kyle, "and I feel pretty good about getting something we can use."

Kohler thought a moment. "Okay. If you need me to run any leads through investigative channels, you have my direct number. Call no matter the time. Governor Clifton has told me to make this my top priority which means I will give you any support you need to get me in touch with the leader of that group."

Andy Kohler rose, walked to his second-floor office window overlooking the park, and gazed out at the serenity below. The park was so peaceful at the end of the day when it was empty. He turned and addressed Kyle and me. "Our arrangement must remain confidential. If anyone were to find out I was using official channels to inquire about the demonstrators it could be viewed as a violation of their civil rights."

"Totally understandable," I said, even though I planned to dig everything I could out of him to save Megan.

Kohler strode to the door and opened it, signaling our meeting was over. Kyle and I left Kohler's office, our mission clear, our arsenal better stocked than when the day had begun.

Chapter Eleven
Albany, NY
June 30, 5:53 PM

Phil Crowley sat on a park bench, head bowed, trying to look like he was napping. Through slitted eyes he studied Kyle Fitzpatrick and the stranger with him as they exited the Capitol building and casually walked across West Capitol Park. They paused to discuss something, then proceeded, eventually exiting the park. Crowley slipped a cell phone from the back pocket of his ratty jeans, dialed a number, and waited impatiently for an answer.

"Pick me up. He's on the move. And he's got a friend," was all he said before abruptly ending the call. Crowley rose, stretched, then fell in well behind the two men. A block later, he watched as they got into a green Jeep Wrangler with the stranger at the wheel. The vehicle pulled into the late-day traffic on Washington Avenue.

At that same instant an older model, well-traveled blue Ford Taurus pulled to the curb and stopped just long enough for Crowley to slide into the passenger seat. The Taurus, with Tony Zacarelli at the wheel, pulled away from the curb, tailing the Jeep.

Fitzpatrick was asking too many people about Gregory Rockwell and his mission. Rockwell wanted Fitzpatrick followed and, if necessary, dealt with.

And I'm just the guy to deal with him, thought Crowley, with a broad smile.

Chapter Twelve
Albany, NY
June 30, 7:02 PM

"How's the meal, boys?"

Kyle and I glanced up from our dinner plates to see Tommy Griesau, ever-present bar rag draped over his left shoulder. We had decided to catch dinner at *Tommy G's* and get our plan together for the next day.

"Hey, Tommy," Kyle managed around a bite of perfectly cooked steak. "Excellent as always."

I swallowed a mouthful of cold frothy draft beer and returned my tall glass to the table. "I swear, Tommy, best food in the city."

"Thanks, boys," Griesau said. "You need anything else, just holler." Tommy Griesau continued his circuit of the packed dining room, stopping to trade pleasantries with guests.

"So what's our next move?" Kyle asked.

"I've got a few ideas on—" At that moment my cell phone chimed. "Hold on a second. I've been waiting for this call." Kyle stopped eating and listened.

"Right. Sure thing." I glanced at my watch. "Yeah,

9:30 tonight is fine. See you then, Beth. I owe you big time." I slipped the phone into my pocket.

"Well?"

"That was a friend of mine at the local all-news television station. She said we could stop by at 9:30 tonight and go through all the file footage of demonstrators at the park for the past month. We need to get a picture of Gregory for Kohler. This is going to be more than a two-man job."

"But he said he couldn't get involved in tracking him down."

"He will when I tell him about Megan."

"Is that wise?"

"Once Kohler knows there's a hostage involved, he'll have no recourse but to get involved. We put a picture of this jerk in law enforcement's hands and blanket the park, along with anywhere else we think he could be."

"And if Kohler says no?" Kyle asked.

"Then we threaten to blackmail him by telling our story through social media, newspapers, television stations, radio, whoever the hell will listen. I'll make damn sure he puts all the power he has behind rescuing Megan."

"But what if—"

I angled my fork toward Kyle. "I told you I would get her back safely. And no one, I mean no one, is going to get in my way."

* * *

Phil Crowley and Tony Zacarelli sat in the darkened interior of the blue Ford Taurus parked within sight of the green Jeep Wrangler they had been tailing. Crowley checked the time on his watch.

"They gotta come outta there soon," he said.

"Wish we'd picked up something to eat," Zacarelli

said. His stomach emitted a rumble.

Crowley suddenly straightened up in his seat. "Here we go," he said. Zacarelli started the engine. As soon as the Jeep pulled out into the street they edged out of their parking spot and followed at a discreet distance. Once again, the chase was on.

Chapter Thirteen
Albany, NY
June 30, 11:24 PM

I paced behind the desk at the local all-news television station. Kyle sat hunched over a large video screen. Pouring through endless videos of past demonstrations around the Capitol was tedious, mind-numbing work, and I wasn't even doing it, just observing Kyle. I rubbed my tired eyes.

"Gotcha, you sonofabitch!" Kyle shot out of his seat. "There he is, Rick!" He jabbed a finger at the figure frozen on the screen.

I studied the image. Not the best but it would give us something to hand to Kohler. "Beth!" I yelled. My contact at the news station rushed into the video room. "Can you blow this guy up and clean up the image?"

"I'll give it my best shot."

"Great. I'll need a physical copy and a second copy on a flash drive," I said. "How long for you to work your magic?"

"Can you give me about twenty minutes?"

"Sounds good." I turned to Kyle. "While Beth is

working on that, you scan the rest of the footage for a better image."

"On it, Rick." Kyle dropped back into the seat and studied the images scrolling across the screen. His energy level seemed to have skyrocketed.

I watched these two people working hard to save the life of another person. I knew we still had a long way to go to get Megan back but at least now the devil had a face. We would grab a couple hours of sleep, then cruise the park tomorrow while trying to draft Andy Kohler as an active member of our group.

* * *

It was almost midnight by the time the two men stepped out through the front door of the television station. Tony Zacarelli woke a dozing Phil Crowley with a smack to the shoulder.

"What?"

Zacarelli pointed to the two men entering the Jeep. They started their vehicle and once again began their stealthy pursuit. The Jeep dropped Fitzpatrick off at a tiny Cape-style home then drove off.

"What do you think?" Zacarelli asked.

"I think we go get some sleep and report to the boss first thing in the morning," Crowley said. "And now we know where this guy lives."

"What about his friend?"

"This is the only guy we're worried about right now," Crowley said. "If the other guy becomes a problem, then we deal with him too." He stretched and yawned. "Drop me off at my place. I'll buzz you in the morning and we'll start this dance again."

The lights of the Taurus came to life and the vehicle disappeared into the night.

Chapter Fourteen
Abandoned farm
Thirteen miles southeast of Albany, NY
July 1, 9:51 AM

Megan Fitzpatrick's throat was raw, courtesy of hours of futile screaming for help. No one heard her cries. No one came to her rescue. She sat quietly on a tattered wool blanket, the only thing separating her butt from the dirt floor in the small structure where she was held captive. She leaned against a rough wooden post, one of many supporting the tall roof. The young woman brushed her raven black bangs out of her deep green eyes and looked around the building. Warm sunlight leaked through countless gaps in the old wood plank walls and splashed on the dirt floor. There was a double door leading in but not one single window. She never heard any sounds from outside, other than the occasional chirp of birds. No vehicles passing by or aircraft flying overhead. She felt she must be far out in the countryside, somewhere beyond the suburbs.

Megan had no idea how long she had been here. The people who had grabbed and dumped her in this place had taken her cell phone and watch. Had it been a day? Maybe two since she was abducted? They left a cooler with bottled water, a variety of protein and energy bars, and bags of dried fruit. She could relieve herself in a far corner of the structure, albeit at the end of a long length of rusty chain attached to a very tight shackle on her right ankle. The other end of the chain was looped around the sturdy post and secured by a padlock.

Megan drained the remaining water from the plastic bottle, then angrily flung it into the pile of other empties and food wrappers. The warm liquid did little to soothe her sore throat. She closed her eyes and tried to figure out how and why she came to be a prisoner here, wherever *here* was. For what seemed like the millionth time she went over everything that had happened to her recently trying to determine if there was something that had triggered this event; once again she came to the conclusion that her boring life gave no clues. There had been nothing out of the ordinary. Nothing at all. Except...Gregory? Was he related to this? But how? Why?

Frustrated, she tore at the chain anchoring her to the support and began to scream again.

* * *

Megan Fitzpatrick was a paralegal at a downtown Albany law firm. As she did on most beautiful days, Megan spent her lunch hour sitting on a park bench in Albany's West Capitol Park observing the latest protest outside the Capitol building.

She first met Gregory Rockwell on a warm, sunny Friday. He introduced himself as Gregory No Last Name. She thought that was a bit strange but didn't push it since he seemed so nice, even charming, when he sat down next to her and struck up a conversation. As an attractive, young woman she was used to getting hit on, but there was something different about him, something sincere.

Rockwell wore a black sweatshirt, the hood up, and dark sunglasses masking his eyes. Megan was cautious, as you never knew who might approach you in the large park packed with people in the shadow of the state capitol. He seemed so at ease with her that after a few minutes his dark glasses came off and his hood dropped onto his wide shoulders. Their conversation centered on the demonstration, politics, and Governor Clifton. He did ask a few personal questions. Megan was surprised to find they had a lot in common.

When her lunch hour was over she rose from the bench and explained she had enjoyed their conversation but had to get back to work. Rockwell said he also enjoyed his short time with her and hoped to run into her again.

"If the weather is nice, this is the bench where I park it Monday through Friday, noon until 1:00 P.M.," Megan said with a grin.

"That's good to know." Rockwell smiled. "I look forward to continuing our political discussions." When Megan didn't reply right away, Rockwell sensed her disappointment that he was only drawn to her because of politics. He quickly added, "Among other things, of course."

"Of course." Megan strode off toward One Commerce Plaza. She had to admit, there may have been a small bounce in her step. Megan couldn't help but think how amazing Gregory Rockwell's hazel eyes were. They seemed to look right into her soul. And he was handsome in a rugged sort of way. Megan planned to be on that park bench the following Monday come hell or high water.

After an excruciatingly long weekend, Megan found herself rushing to her favorite park bench on Monday at noon. To her surprise, there sat Gregory No Last Name, sunglasses off and hood down, a few wildflowers in hand, waiting for her. They seemed to pick up right where they left off. This went on for the entire week and by Friday he popped the question, but not the *would you like to go on a date* question. He asked if she would be interested in joining his protest group. This set her back a bit; it was not at all what she was expecting. Looking for an out, she explained she had a full-time job and really couldn't dedicate the time. Rockwell pressured her with stronger talk of mild violence, if necessary, to bring about the changes they both knew had to happen. He said they had big things planned that would change the political climate in New York. What he had tried to show as flexing his muscles instead set off an alarm in her head. And then a brilliant thought came to her, and she now wondered if it was that very same brilliant thought that had a hand in the predicament she currently found herself in.

"I may know the perfect person for your group. My older brother Kyle. He sounds just like you. He's a strong individual who's against everything Governor Clifton stands for."

In truth, she was winging it, setting Gregory Rockwell up to be the object of her brother's first big news exposé, a story that could launch Kyle Fitzpatrick into that elusive investigative reporting career that always seemed just out of his reach. To be inside a protest group preaching violence in its infancy would make a great story.

"I'm disappointed you won't be joining our grand campaign," Rockwell said. He hesitated, as if debating something in his head. "If your brother is anything like you, I'd be happy to hear what he has to say."

"You won't be disappointed," she said.

* * *

The first time Kyle Fitzpatrick and Gregory Rockwell met they connected perfectly. Megan left them together on the park bench and set off for her office. Her job here was done as far as she was concerned. She was happy to find out Gregory No Last Name was not worth getting interested in before she had invested too much time. *Oh well, it might be time to pick out a different bench in a different park.*

* * *

"So, Gregory, Megan tells me you have some big things planned. If it means knocking Clifton off her freaking throne you can count me in." Gregory Rockwell was so impressed with Kyle's opening line that he decided to feel him out—without revealing too much.

They met three more times before Rockwell felt comfortable enough to invite Kyle into his group. The two men sat on their usual park bench deeply discussing how far Kyle was willing to go to defend his beliefs when someone shouted.

"Hey, Kyle!"

A well-dressed man in his mid-50s traversed the green lawn. Kyle jumped up from the bench and rushed to intercept the man before he got too close.

"I can't talk right now," he whispered, hoping Rockwell wouldn't hear him.

"What do you mean you can't talk right now? Not even to me, your good buddy, who may have a line on a reporting job for you?" He made no attempt to keep his voice down.

Kyle glanced over his shoulder to see Rockwell, now with his sunglasses on and hood up, staring at him from the bench. The days he spent laying down the foundation for a good story may have just gone down the drain.

"Just go. I'll call you later." He turned his friend around and nudged him from behind. The man walked off, a look of irritation on his face. On top of everything else, Kyle may have just lost another shot at a reporting job. He returned to the bench and took up his position next to Rockwell.

"Sorry about that. Not sure what that jerk was talking about."

"No problem," Rockwell said. "Couldn't hear him anyway with all the protestors shouting up at the governor's windows."

Kyle relaxed a bit. It sounded to him like his friend's interruption was nothing more than a near miss. Gregory hadn't heard anything. The story was still a go. He settled back into his character. "Not that the bitch gives a good goddamn." They both chuckled.

But Gregory Rockwell had heard every word and while he continued their conversation, he was also working on another plan, one that would keep Kyle Fitzpatrick from uttering a word about his group to anyone.

* * *

Gregory Rockwell had let his guard down with Megan Fitzpatrick. That very first time he looked into her eyes he was reminded of someone. Someone long gone. Megan had the same sparkling eyes and soft warm smile his mother had had before she self-destructed. He had almost blown the entire plan against Clifton because of that. Almost, but he would get it back on track.

The next morning Gregory Rockwell unleashed his inner circle on Megan Fitzpatrick in the parking lot of an apartment complex on the outskirts of Albany where she rented a cozy one-bedroom. The sun had barely crept over the horizon as Megan locked her front door and strode to her car. Her mind was preoccupied going over the list of items she needed to attend to as soon as she got to work. It was shaping up to be a hectic day.

Car keys in hand, she squeezed between her red Toyota and a rust-streaked white van with blacked-out windows. As soon as her back was turned, the side door of the van flew open. Phil Crowley and Tony Zacarelli, both with bandanas covering their faces, dragged her into the van and slammed the door shut. They pinned Megan face-down on the truck bed while they wrestled her wrists and ankles into plastic cuffs. Zacarelli stuffed a gag into Megan's mouth and pushed a dark pillowcase over her head as Crowley drove the van out of the lot.

The old van bounced and swayed for almost an hour before they arrived at their destination—an abandoned farm, thirteen miles southeast of Albany. Megan was carried out, unceremoniously dumped in a small building, and chained like an animal. And they never uttered a single word except that one of the men said she would be released unharmed in a few days as long as she didn't give them any trouble.

Now she looked around her small prison, terrified and confused, wondering what the hell was going on and who these people were. And if she would live to find out.

Chapter Fifteen
Albany, NY
July 1, 12:11 PM

Kyle and I had been crisscrossing West Capitol Park for the last two hours checking the faces of countless passersby and demonstrators against the photos we discreetly palmed. No sign of the elusive Gregory No Last Name as of yet. Our second day searching for the man we believed held Megan Fitzpatrick's life in his hands was no more productive than the first. Out of frustration, we took a chance and asked some of the food vendors lining the park if they had seen him. The response was no better. This guy was nowhere to be found.

Our paths met by the large fountain in the park.

"Well?" I said.

"Not a goddamn thing." Kyle looked all around him, willing Gregory to step out of the crowd. "We have to find this guy now, Rick. We're running out of time."

I needed to keep Kyle busy, focused. "Tell you what, Kyle. You go over and wander around the Empire State Plaza. Maybe he's hanging over there where he can observe what's going on here from a distance."

"I don't know, Rick, do you really think—"

"Trust me, Kyle. Okay?" He nodded. "I'll continue to walk around here. If he's here, we'll find him. And if he's not here, we'll still find him. Somehow, somewhere." Once again, Kyle nodded. "We'll get her back. I swear."

"If I didn't trust you, Rick, I wouldn't have come to you for help." He turned and jogged toward the adjacent Empire State Plaza.

I watched Kyle as he headed off, then stared down at the picture of Gregory clutched in my hand. "Where are you, you sonofabitch?" I scanned the faces of the crowd around me and was about to set off crisscrossing the park when I froze, my eyes locking on Kyle's figure receding in the distance.

I yanked the cell phone from my pocket and dialed Kyle's number. "Come on, pick up, pick up." The call went to voicemail. "Kyle, it's Rick. I think you've picked up a tail. Jeans, black jacket, red ball cap. I'm coming your way." Either Kyle had his phone turned off or he couldn't hear it ringing above the mid-day din of the patrons clogging the park. I crammed the phone back in my pocket and rushed off after him.

* * *

Phil Crowley had been observing Fitzpatrick and the stranger from a safe distance as they wound their way through the park. When Fitzpatrick split from the stranger, he grabbed his cell phone and called Tony Zacarelli, who was somewhere out of sight on the other side of the park. He instructed Zacarelli to tail Fitzpatrick while he kept an eye on the other guy.

Crowley watched with interest as Fitzpatrick's buddy pulled out his cell phone, spoke for a few seconds, then took off after Fitzpatrick. Or was he now following

Zacarelli? Phil Crowley fell in line behind Fitzpatrick's buddy. This might be his opportunity to find out who the mystery man was up close.

* * *

I exited West Capitol Park, crossed State Street, and entered the north end of the Empire State Plaza. After scanning the area, I located Kyle halfway down the plaza moving quickly. The man I had seen taking off after Kyle was still in tow. I hurried to catch up. This had to be more than just a coincidence.

The south boundary of the plaza butted up to Madison Avenue, ending slightly above street level. Two sets of stairs led down to the avenue below. I watched as Kyle hustled down the set on the right, disappearing from view. The guy tailing him was hot in pursuit, not even trying to hide it now. He also disappeared from view as he hit the stairs. I was puzzled as to why Kyle would leave the plaza instead of circling it like we had discussed. *Where the hell was he going?* I broke into a flat out run trying to catch up to the two men.

Vaulting down the stairs two steps at a time, I skidded to a halt when I hit the sidewalk below. The guy who had been tailing Kyle was now pinned against a stone wall, Kyle's clenched hands full of the man's black jacket.

* * *

"Why are you following me?" Kyle yelled. "Who the hell are you?" When his questions were met with silence he yanked the guy away from the wall and slammed him back against it. "Answer me, you bastard!"

"Kyle!" I struggled to haul him off the stranger. "Take it easy!"

"What's your problem, man?" The stranger went after Kyle, who responded in kind, rushing forward.

Crushed between the two combatants, I shoved them apart again.

"Knock it off!" I said, one hand against my friend's chest, holding him back, the other hand pointing at the stranger. "And you back off! Why are you following him?"

The stranger thumbed his ball cap back and scratched his head. "What the hell are you talking about? I'm not following him. I don't even know him!"

Kyle pushed against my hand, still resting on his chest. "The hell you're not. Where's my sister?"

"Your sis—what are you, crazy? I don't know your sister."

"You better not be screwing with us," I said.

He looked around, his eyes stopping on a bus stop sign. "Hey, man. I'm running to catch a bus, okay? Maybe you're screwing with *me.* How about I call a cop to straighten this out? And maybe arrest your ass."

If he's lying, he's a damn good actor, I thought, *And we are standing right next to a bus stop.* Quite a few people looked on, presumably waiting for a bus. If we lingered any longer the cell phones would come out and the videos would end up on the internet. "No reason to bother the cops. My buddy here is under a lot of stress. What say we all just go our separate ways and forget this ever happened."

The stranger glanced at Kyle, then tugged his hat down to his brow. "Watch your step. Next time you might not be so lucky." He rammed his hands into his pockets and skulked down Madison Avenue toward downtown Albany.

"What tipped you off?" I asked when the stranger was gone.

"I heard my phone beeping once I got away from the

crowd. I listened to your voicemail, then led him down here and made my move."

"It's possible we made a mistake."

Kyle stared at the receding figure through angry eyes. "So you believe that guy?"

"Let it go, Kyle. We're both getting edgy." I slapped him on the shoulder. "C'mon. We've got work to get back to." We trotted up the stairs and traversed the Empire State Plaza on our way back to West Capitol Park. I fully believed this Gregory guy had to come out of his hole eventually, and when he did, I would be right there to grab him by his neck and choke the truth out of him.

* * *

Crowley had hidden at the rear of the crowd surrounding the bus stop, silently observing the scuffle between Zacarelli and the two men. The three participants of the shoving match eventually separated and went off in opposite directions. As soon as the bus stop throng began to dissipate, Crowley called Zacarelli.

"Meet me in Academy Park. I'll be near the corner of Eagle and Elk Streets."

"On my way."

"And try not to get caught this time."

Less than ten minutes later Tony Zacarelli approached Phil Crowley at the agreed upon rendezvous point. Crowley didn't look happy.

"You're lucky those guys didn't push it," Crowley said. "You could have blown it all up on us." A grin spread across Zacarelli's whisker-stubbled face. Crowley was clearly annoyed. "What's so funny?"

"Just this." Zacarelli pulled a black business card case from his jacket pocket. He tossed the case to Crowley.

Crowley looked inside. "Are you freakin' kidding me?"

"In case you've forgotten, being a pickpocket is just one of my many talents," Zacarelli said. "I lifted it from Fitzpatrick's buddy when he got between us."

"Well, I'll be," Crowley said. Now they knew who the guy hanging around with Fitzpatrick was. "I need to let the boss know right away. Looks like we have Rick Patterson, Private Investigator, on our asses now too." Crowley smiled at Zacarelli. "Seems we got ourselves a brand new dance going on."

* * *

Kyle once again took up his patrol of West Capitol Park. After another hour he still had nothing to show for it. The crowd was thinning out, even the demonstrators were calling it a day. At the same time, I was on the phone with Andy Kohler. I told the press secretary about finding a picture of the person we believed to be the leader of the group causing Governor Clifton so much grief. I also told him we had no luck finding the guy. I asked if Kohler could take the picture and run it through whatever channels he could to point us in the right direction. My plea for help was denied. Kohler reiterated that any interference by the administration might be looked upon as harassing the demonstrators' civil rights.

"Well?" Kyle said. "Is he going to help us?"

I slipped my phone into my pocket. "Says he can't. Something about infringing on their civil rights." I let out an aggravated breath. "Looks like it's still you and me, buddy."

"Well, that's just great," Kyle said. "After all, we've had such good luck the last two days." He was justifiably angry. "We've only got three days left. Maybe."

The park was beginning to empty out. Soon it would be vacant, and there would be no one else to ask about Gregory. *Think, Rick, think. Something is going to happen in three days. You're running out of time. Megan is running out of time.* I looked at Kyle. "We don't have time to be stealthy any more. We finish out the day walking the streets around here showing this guy's picture to everyone we see. First thing tomorrow we go kick down Andy Kohler's door and blackmail him if we have to. I'm done screwing around."

* * *

"Yeah. His name is Rick Patterson. His card says he's a private investigator." Phil Crowley was speaking with Gregory Rockwell on his cell phone.

Rockwell had wisely stayed out of sight since Megan Fitzpatrick had been taken. He still refused to refer to her abduction as a kidnapping. He wasn't looking for a ransom and fully planned to release her unharmed after the event on the USS *Slater* concluded. "Stick with these guys. And make sure the rest of our people know enough not to say a word about me."

"On it, boss." Crowley turned to Zacarelli. "Let's go. We keep these guys in sight." They strode off, keeping a safe distance behind Rick Patterson and Kyle Fitzpatrick.

Chapter Sixteen
USS *Slater* (DE-766)
Hudson River, NY
July 1, 3:52 PM

The *Slater* made her way back to Albany on the Hudson River under a cloudless azure sky. The old warship was being nudged along at a speed of eight knots by a pair of tugboats at her stern, the *Katie Ann* on her port quarter, the *Joanna Lynn* on her starboard quarter. She looked glorious wearing her newly applied wartime camouflage paint, the colors a mix of grays and blues covering her hull. Creamy white waves curled away from her steel bow as she approached the Esopus Meadows Lighthouse.

An endless stream of small boats had buzzed the *Slater* since her departure from New York City, the well-wishers sounding their horns and waving American flags at the incredible sight from a time before most of them were born. Throngs of cheering people dotted the tree-lined shores and waved from high spots all along the Hudson River as the last-of-its-kind vessel slowly made her way north through the tranquil water. The crew of twenty-four aboard the warship gratefully yelled their thanks and waved back at the spectators.

One of the crewmembers aboard the *Slater* was not in the mood to take part in the ongoing festivities. Carter Anson leaned on one of the portside lifeline stanchions opposite the stairs leading up to the boat deck. He watched the Esopus Meadows Lighthouse getting closer off the ship's bow, a scowl on his face. He was never supposed to be on the vessel heading back to Albany.

Anson had been tagged at the last minute to ride with the crew of the *Slater*. He was to keep an eye on the welds below deck in case there were any problems that had been missed during the final inspection. He had done his best to argue the point with his boss that everything was fine, that there were others who could go along on the ship's return voyage, but his protests fell on deaf ears and, as lead welder, he was drafted for the journey. Now he needed to get off the ship as soon as they docked in Albany and race back to Staten Island. He had to disappear before whatever was in the three rucksacks he had hidden below deck was discovered and traced back to him.

The management team for the *Slater* had arranged transportation back to New York City for Carter Anson but it would take a day or two. His contact in Albany, however, had made covert arrangements to get him back immediately. Anson would be hitching a ride on a small delivery truck transporting local farm produce to White Plains where a connecting ride would get him back to the city.

"Yeah, just make damn sure you got my return transportation arranged as soon as I step off this garbage scow," Anson growled into his cell phone. "This was never part of the plan."

"Calm down before you blow it. Everything is all set here," Gregory Rockwell reassured him. Rockwell was currently preparing his people for the next demonstration against Governor Helen Clifton. Anson could hear the confusing jumble of voices in the background. "All you have to do is get off the ship and meet me where I told you to. Got it?"

"Yeah, I got it." Anson hesitated. "I shouldn't be here, you know."

"I know. It's no big deal, though. You'll be on your way back before the ship is even tied up for the night," Rockwell said. "Trust me."

"I'll trust you when I see the lights of New York City again." Out of the corner of his eye he noticed one of the crewmen approaching. "Someone's coming." Anson jammed the phone in the hip pocket of his weathered jeans. The crewman stopped before he reached Anson and leaned over the railing. Esopus Meadows Lighthouse slid past on their port side, its white clapboard siding and red mansard roof gleaming in the bright sunlight.

Anson glanced at his watch. With any luck, and if the tides, river flow, and river traffic were in his favor, the *Slater* would be tying up in Albany in another seven hours. And in seven hours and one minute he would be speeding back to New York City, then to parts unknown.

Chapter Seventeen
Albany, NY
July 1, 11:23 PM

Carter Anson watched from the shadows on the deck of the *Slater* as one of the tugs nudged the old warship toward its dock in the Port of Albany. As soon as the *Slater* was secured he planned to get off her and disappear. What Anson found astonishing was that it was almost midnight and the dock was jammed with people welcoming the old World War II relic back home.

The waterfront was crawling with people, almost every one of them waving an American flag or holding up a homemade placard. Wall-to-wall people, all clapping and cheering. Young, old, children on their parents' shoulders, all mixed in with a few World War II vets in ill-fitting uniforms at the front of the crowd supported by walkers and wheelchairs, tears in their eyes. There was even a band from a local high school playing something patriotic and acting as if it was a sunny afternoon on a football field instead of near-midnight at Albany's port.

Carter Anson was startled by a series of loud bangs. The sky above the *Slater*'s welcoming crowd lit up, the well-wishers on the dock cast in blue, then white, and finally red. Fireworks! It was then he saw news vans behind the crowd, their transmission booms reaching up into the darkness, flashing pictures of the warship to countless viewers. Along with his image. Anson had a feeling in his gut that it was going to be damn near impossible to slip away unnoticed.

By the time lines were thrown and cables secured, almost ninety minutes had passed, and all that time the crowd kept their vigil, cheering and waving their flags. And the band played on, oblivious to the horror buried deep within the *Slater*'s hull.

Ninety minutes of waiting to jump ship. Ninety minutes of trying to stay undetected in the shadows. Ninety minutes of staring at the crowd. In the end, ninety minutes is what it took to convince Carter Anson that he could not go through with it. He scanned the crowd, lingering on some of the faces. The spectrum ran all the way from small children to old veterans, all of them innocent. They did not deserve to be exposed to what was hidden aboard the *Slater*.

Anson backed away from the lifeline, disappearing from view in the dark area below the superstructure. He fumbled his cell phone out of his jeans pocket and pressed the number for Gregory Rockwell. It was answered immediately.

"I see the ship is back. You ready to get off and get going?" Anson was silent. "Carter? You there?"

Carter Anson hesitated, not sure how to say what he had to. "I can't do it," he said. "I thought I could but I can't."

"Yeah, you can. And you will. You're just a little rattled right now. Meet me and we'll straighten it all out."

"I looked in one of the rucksacks you gave me to

hide." He cleared his throat. "I thought you were smuggling drugs or something. You never said anything about goddamn explosives." Silence from Rockwell. "I'm going below while the crew is busy topside. I'm going to remove them all and dump them overboard."

"Don't do anything until I get there, okay?"

"I've got to make my move while everyone is on deck." Anson knew as soon as he was face-to-face with Rockwell, the man would do his damnedest to browbeat him into proceeding with the plan.

"Is it the money? I can get you more if that's what it is."

"No, I don't want your money. This is wrong, just wrong." Anson closed his eyes. "The dock is packed with people. Kids, old war vets, just regular people. Probably the same people who are gonna be here July 4th. They don't deserve to be hurt. They're innocent."

"Listen to me. I—"

Anson cut Rockwell off. "I won't do it!"

Rockwell changed tactics. "I will be there in less than five minutes. Just wait for me. I'll hop aboard when no one is watching and help you."

"I stashed them all away, I can get them out of there myself."

"And do what with them? You just might set one off." Rockwell spoke louder now. "Please. Just wait for me. If you're not going through with it at least we can make sure we don't set them off by mistake and kill everyone."

"I don't know," Anson said.

"You might be right. Maybe this was a mistake. Just wait for me."

"Five minutes, and then I move on my own."

Rockwell hit the cancel button on his cell phone. He

had been lurking a few blocks from the dock waiting for Anson's call. Now he was flat out running to get to the dock. Another bump in the road to deal with, just like he had had with Megan Fitzpatrick. He took care of her. He would take care of Carter Anson too. And then he would take care of her highness, Governor Helen Clifton.

Chapter Eighteen
Albany, NY
July 1, 11:39 PM

It took an agonizing sixteen minutes for Gregory Rockwell to get to the *Slater*, tied port side to the dock. He wormed his way to the front of the packed crowd, but saw no sign of Carter Anson. The sonofabitch was probably making good on his threat to drag the rucksacks from their hiding places and heave them over the side.

Suddenly someone emerged from a hatch near the quarterdeck. He couldn't tell if it was Anson. The figure darted toward the bow of the ship and slipped across the deck to the starboard side, all the time staying in the shadows.

And it sure looked like the person was carrying one of his rucksacks. Was that Anson with one of his bombs? Had he gotten them all out yet? Rockwell could not wait any longer.

The band began playing and, as a few fireworks lit up the sky and captured everyone's attention, he grabbed a large coil of rope lying on the dock, threw it over his shoulder to conceal his face, then pushed his way across the gangway and onto the ship. He was at the end of the gangway ready to set foot on the deck when someone shouted at him from behind.

"Hey! Where ya goin' with that?" Rockwell turned, shielding his face with the coil of rope. A portly middle-aged man in denims, a blue chambray work shirt, and a navy-blue baseball cap sporting a silver silhouette of the USS *Slater* approached across the gangway. "Yeah, you. Where ya goin'?"

Rockwell thought fast. "Carter asked me to grab this and bring it to him. No idea why. I just take orders from him." The man was getting too close. Rockwell didn't wait for him, instead he turned quickly and scurried off.

The man stood in the middle of the gangway, baseball cap in hand, scratching his head. "Okay, then. Go ahead and get that to him." His voice trailed off. He figured the man mentioned Carter Anson by name so he must know him.

Rockwell hurried toward the bow and cut over to the starboard side of the ship. He came face to face with Carter Anson getting ready to drop the rucksack over the side. The men locked eyes. Rockwell dropped the coil of rope.

Rockwell stabbed a finger at the rucksack hanging precariously over the lifeline. "Is that all of them?" he demanded. Anson was noticeably nervous, or maybe he was terrified, either from the bomb in his hands or facing off with Rockwell.

"I couldn't wait for you," said Anson.

"I asked if that was all of them."

"This is the first one." As if to justify his actions, Anson added, "You said five minutes. I couldn't wait for you."

Rockwell glared at Anson. "Do not drop it over the

side. You could set it off and kill everyone." He held his hand out. "Give it to me." Anson balanced the rucksack on the lifeline. "I said, give it to me. Now. I have to disarm it first." A long, tense moment passed in silence. "Carter, just put it on the deck." Anson's hands shook as he lowered the black rucksack to the deck, then stepped away from it. "Where was this one hidden?" Rockwell asked as he moved toward Anson and the rucksack.

"The refrigerated storeroom."

"So the other two are where I asked you to hide them?"

"Yes."

"And you didn't mess with them?"

"No. This is the only one I looked in. You can take the money back. I don't want anything to do with this."

"I appreciate your honesty, Carter. I truly do." Rockwell stepped up to the lifeline and looked out upon the still water, lit by the fireworks. "Let's just take a deep breath and calm down, then we'll get the other rucksacks."

Anson gripped the lifeline with both hands, bowed his head, and closed his eyes. "I'm glad you understand. I wasn't sure what you might do when I—" Before Anson could say another word, something crashed into the side of his head, knocking him to his knees. He wavered for a second before toppling over.

Rockwell stood over Anson, waiting for him to move. Carter Anson would never move again courtesy of the crushing blow Rockwell had delivered from a three-foot length of steel pipe he had found leaning against the superstructure behind him. Rockwell stood motionless gripping the pipe. His heart beat so fast, so hard, that it felt like it was trying to smash its way out of his chest. He felt Anson's neck for a pulse. Nothing. Another loose end dealt with. Now he had to return the rucksack to its hiding place below deck before—

"Hey!" It was the same crewman he'd slipped by when he came aboard. "Who's over there?" The guy was so far away he really couldn't see anything beyond Rockwell's silhouette by the lifeline.

"It's okay," Rockwell shouted back. "Just checking out the view."

"Well look sharp! A news crew is coming aboard in a few minutes."

"Gotcha." He watched as the crewman disappeared. Thoughts raced through Rockwell's head. He looked down at the rucksack, at Anson's lifeless body, at his flawless plan falling apart. He grabbed Anson under his arms and heaved him up, leaning him over the lifeline. He waited nervously for the next flurry of fireworks. As soon as they went off the band played again. Rockwell unceremoniously dropped Anson's body over the side, followed by the bloody pipe. The exploding fireworks and loud music covered the sound of the body and murder weapon entering the water.

There was no time to get below deck and hide the rucksack. Two bombs would have to do. He shouldered the rucksack, once again grabbed the rope to shield his face, and strode to the gangway. He lingered in the shadows, and when the next flurry of fireworks held everyone's attention, he hustled over the gangway, dropped the rope on the dock, and ran as fast as he could down the darkened streets around the *Slater.*

Chapter Nineteen
Abandoned farm
Thirteen miles southeast of Albany, NY
July 2, 1:53 AM

One of Gregory Rockwell's achievements had been to turn his followers into an unknowing smokescreen to hide behind in his quest to destroy Governor Helen Clifton. Unwittingly, they also served as his personal motor pool, happy to lend their charismatic leader whatever transportation they had. That's where the white van Crowley and Zacarelli had used to snatch Megan Fitzpatrick came from as well as the car he had borrowed to run tonight's errand.

The small, banged-up vehicle coasted with its engine off, finally coming to a stop in the shadows behind the small building where Megan Fitzpatrick was a prisoner. This far from any city lights, the sky above the surrounding wilderness was black and cloudless, hosting a thin crescent moon and a sprinkling of flickering pinpoints of white light. He had chosen this abandoned farm wisely; there was no one around for miles. Rockwell eased the driver's door open and unfolded himself from the cramped car, listening to the silence.

"Sounds like the bitch finally stopped screaming," said Phil Crowley. He stepped from the passenger side and yanked the black rucksack from the rear seat.

"Be careful!" Rockwell said. "And don't call her that again."

"Hey, no problem, boss. I just—"

"She hasn't done anything to deserve that, okay? We follow the plan, then cut her loose. Keep it civil." Rockwell snatched a flashlight and a small grease-stained paper bag from the dashboard. Crowley held his hands up in mock surrender, then shouldered the rucksack.

Phil Crowley was truly a wild card. Not only was he one of Rockwell's most important co-conspirators, he was also the only one possessing the expertise to configure the three bombs. Rockwell never asked how he came to know so much about explosives, and didn't want to know. Problem was, Crowley was a little too robust in his role as Rockwell's right-hand man, prompting Rockwell to keep him on a short leash.

Rockwell dialed a series of numbers into the combination lock that secured an old rusty chain across the entrance, then slipped inside. Crowley followed.

"Who's there?" Megan Fitzpatrick shouted from the darkness. When no one answered, she began to scream. "Please, help me!"

Rockwell thumbed his flashlight on. "You might as well stop screaming. No one can hear you."

"Gregory? Is that you?"

Rockwell played the bright beam of light over the young woman. Megan struggled to her feet. Somehow she still looked attractive in spite of her being tethered to the support post like a dog for the last few days. There was nothing to be gained by hiding any longer. "Yeah, it's me."

"Please, help me—"

"Sorry things went this way. Just stay quiet and I promise to release you in a few days. You have to trust me."

"You did this to me? You kidnapped me and then chained me up like an animal? Are you crazy? How can I trust you?"

"I will let you go, but only if you behave."

"But why? I'm nobody. I don't have any rich relatives. What do you expect to get by kidnapping me?"

"Silence. That's what I expect to get from you." Megan looked at him, not comprehending. "Or more accurately, *for* you, from your brother."

Now it began to make sense. This must have something to do with Megan's brother, Kyle, trying to infiltrate Gregory's group for a story. "And you think by kidnapping me, he won't say a word about your plans to disrupt Governor Clifton's campaign? That's what all this is about?" Rockwell stared at her in silence. "You sonofabitch! You sick, crazy sonofabitch!" She yanked hard on the chain. "Let me go right now or so help me God when Kyle finds you, I guarantee you'll be sorry!"

Rockwell turned to Phil Crowley and nodded toward a ramshackle workbench, far out of reach of Megan Fitzpatrick's chain. "Take the rucksack and check it out. Make sure the wiring is still okay. And be careful with it." Crowley placed the rucksack on the table and began examining the inside of it with his own flashlight.

"Here," Rockwell said, his tone softening as he tossed Megan the paper bag. She caught it, never taking her eyes off him. "Thought you might like a sandwich."

She looked in the bag, then threw it at him. It hit him in the chest and tumbled to the dirt floor. He never flinched. His voice took on a hard edge. "Suit yourself." He kicked the bag back at her. "Eat, don't eat. I don't really care." The entire time he had stayed just out of reach of her chain. He strode over to the workbench where Crowley was completing his examination.

"It's still good to go," Crowley said. "Any idea where we're gonna plant it?"

"No. We've only got one so we have to be smart and make it count. It should be coordinated with the two hidden on the *Slater*."

A smile crept across Crowley's face. "Have you thought about special delivery air mail?" Rockwell looked at him, a hint of confusion on his face. "Small drones are the thing now, right? You see them on the news all the time with cameras strapped to them. And a lot of businesses are planning to use them to deliver packages." Crowley leaned in conspiratorially and whispered, "I could easily modify this baby and strap her to a drone. We could deliver it at a time and place of our choosing."

Rockwell considered Crowley's proposal. "That could be more dangerous than just planting it somewhere. Might even turn it into a suicide mission for us."

"Hey, boss, no one lives forever, right?"

Even though Phil Crowley had become an essential part of Gregory Rockwell's plan, there didn't seem to be any line he wouldn't cross. Yes, he was in it for the money, but Rockwell felt Crowley might be in this more for the thrill. And that could get them both caught, or even killed, if he didn't get his number two under control.

"I'll think about it," Rockwell said.

"Just so you know, I've already been working on a drone that could do the job easily. She's pretty much ready to go."

"I said I'll think about it." Crowley started to push it,

but Rockwell cut him off with a wave of his hand. "Go ahead and pack up." Rockwell peered over at Megan. She had dropped back to the dirt floor, leaning against the support, her smart business suit dirty and wrinkled. Her knees were up, head bowed in her hands. The bag of food sat untouched near her feet. "I'll be out in a second."

If he had any regrets about this entire scheme, it was that he had to chain up this poor, innocent girl. She didn't deserve it, had nothing to do with it. He might be plotting to murder the governor of New York State but there was still a small flicker of humanity deep inside him. He pulled his tattered family picture from his shirt pocket and stared at it in the flashlight's glow. *But she could blow it all.* He hardened his heart. His parents were innocent too and look where it got them. He rammed the snapshot back in his pocket and stormed out of the building, securing the chain across the door.

Chapter Twenty
Albany, NY
July 2, 7:14 AM

"Hell of a way to start our shift, huh, partner?"

Albany Police Officer Steve Flynn stood tall on the deck of the USS *Slater*, looking out over the Port of Albany. His hands rested on his hips, posing as if he was modeling for a photograph. His partner, Officer Dave Witkowski, leaned over the lifeline of the vintage warship with a telescoping boat hook. He was struggling unsuccessfully to snag the body floating face down in the dirty water on the starboard side of the vessel. Volunteer crew members watched in silence from farther down the lifeline. One of them had spotted the body as the sun came up and called 911. Flynn and Witkowski, on patrol in the area, were dispatched to the scene.

Witkowski stopped momentarily to address Flynn. "I hope you're not working too hard, *partner*."

Flynn frowned. "Somebody has to be the brains of the team." Witkowski shook his head and returned to poking the floater, attempting to at least keep the body from drifting away.

"Where's the goddamn rescue boat?" Witkowski griped. "I can't keep this guy here all freakin' day with this damn pole." He hung precariously over the lifeline. "Not by myself, anyway." A rescue vessel from the Albany Fire Department Marine Unit crept into sight from the direction of the bow. As soon as they pulled alongside the body Witkowski's balancing act would be over.

A few minutes later crewmembers on the 36-foot rescue vessel wrestled the body aboard. One of them yelled up to Flynn and Witkowski to meet them at the boat launch. The two officers piled into their patrol car and drove off, but not before tasking a pair of newly-arrived officers with stringing bright yellow crime-scene tape to safeguard an area of the *Slater*'s deck. The examination of dried blood and other evidence would have to wait until crime scene investigators could get to the ship.

* * *

By the time Flynn and Witkowski arrived at the boat launch, the floater was being offloaded. The detective on site checked the victim's pockets and found a wallet containing a driver's license identifying him as Carter Anson from Brooklyn, New York. He also found a dead cell phone and a soggy black-and-white diagram of what looked to be the cross section of a large ship.

The detective examined the diagram, being careful not to ruin it. Witkowski stared over the detective's shoulder. He pointed a finger at a blurred notation in the lower left corner of the waterlogged paper. "Says right there it's the USS *Slater*."

"Yeah, I see that. This guy may have been connected to the *Slater*. If he was, he could have fallen overboard during the celebration when they arrived last night."

Witkowski was still checking the diagram. "Wonder

what's with those three red Xs."

The detective considered them. "No idea." He took photos of the driver's license and the diagram of the *Slater* with his cell phone, then slipped the items into evidence bags. He forwarded the photos to Flynn and Witkowski's cell phones. "You guys head back to the *Slater* and see if anyone knows him. You can ask them about those Xs if you want, but I'm guessing they're probably nothing. I'll catch up with you over there after I wrap things up here."

* * *

"Sonofabitch," said Pete Franzoni, the middle-aged crew member who had unknowingly addressed Gregory Rockwell as he boarded the ship last night. "That surely is Carter Anson." Murmurs from the rest of the crew members rose in volume.

Flynn held his hands up to silence them. "Who was the last one to see him?"

Franzoni was still fixated on the image of Anson's pale face on Flynn's cell phone. When no one responded, Franzoni spoke up. "Mighta been me."

Flynn pushed through to Franzoni. "What did you see?"

Franzoni thought for moment. "After we tied up I saw him on deck. He was making his way forward and to the starboard side."

"And that was it?" Flynn asked. "He didn't say anything?"

"Not to me. Maybe to that other guy."

"What other guy?" Witkowski called out. His question was met with a glare from Flynn.

"What other guy?" Flynn asked, taking back control of his interview.

"Don't know who he was. Pretty sure he wasn't part of the crew that sailed the old girl home though."

"Tell me about this other guy."

"Not much to tell. It was dark so I didn't really get a good look at him. He was coming over the gangway with a coil of rope over his shoulder. It was kinda blocking his face. I asked him where he was going and he said Carter told him to grab the rope and bring it to him. Said he had no idea why, just that he took orders from him." Franzoni took a moment, then added, "Come to think of it, I don't really know what Carter would have wanted a coil of rope for. He was a welder, you know."

"And that was it?" said Witkowski.

"Maybe it was him I saw after that up toward the bow on the starboard side." Franzoni pointed behind him to the stern. "I was down that way and I thought I saw someone up there." He now turned and pointed toward the spot up on the bow where blood had been found. "I yelled out to whoever it was. It could have been that same guy. He yelled back that he was just admiring the scenery. I said okay and went back to the gangway." Franzoni removed his baseball cap, scratched his head. "That was it. Never saw him again."

Flynn pulled up the photograph of the soggy *Slater* diagram on his cell phone. He held the phone over his head and flashed it around to the crew members. "We found this on Anson's body. Anybody know what these red Xs on this diagram are?"

Once again, Pete Franzoni was the only one to speak out. "Those are spaces down below. I don't know why Carter would have them marked. Nothing there he would have been working on."

"You seem to be the only one who knows what's going on here," Witkowski said.

"I'm lead for this bunch of misfits," Franzoni replied. He slipped a pair of reading glasses from his shirt pocket.

"Can I see that diagram again?" Flynn held up his cell phone. Franzoni put on his glasses and leaned in toward the screen. "Like I said. Nothing there Carter was working on. Nothing there anybody was working on, in fact."

"Think it's worth checking out?" Witkowski asked.

Franzoni shrugged. "It's up to you. Wouldn't take more than a few minutes if you don't mind crawling around down below. Might get your uniform a little dirty."

Flynn glanced at Witkowski. "Go ahead if you want. I'm good right where I am." He looked out over the water at the far shore. "I say we dump this in the detective's lap when he gets here." He snuck a peek at his watch. "If he ever gets here."

Witkowski stuffed his notepad and pen into his pocket and told Franzoni to lead the way. Franzoni picked up a flashlight, then focused on a young man near the front. "Hey, Danny Sauer. Grab a tool bag and join the party." He disappeared through a hatch with Witkowski and Sauer in tow.

* * *

First stop for the three men was the refrigerated storeroom, known as the reefer deck, located just forward of the mess decks. "Here's the first marking on the diagram, near as I can tell," said Franzoni. The space contained refrigeration compressors, electric motors, and condensers. "What should we be looking for?"

"You got me," Witkowski replied. "I guess anything that looks out of place or shouldn't be here." Franzoni and Sauer went through the entire room, checking behind the equipment and overhead conduits, and removing any access panels they could get to while Witkowski stood and watched. Their search revealed nothing out of the ordinary. The three men moved on to the second area designated by a red X on the diagram.

* * *

Witkowski looked on as Franzoni and Sauer examined the forward motor room (B-2). Sauer was on his toes snaking his arm above the control panel when he stopped and called out, "Something's up here, Pete."

"Get your arm outta there and let me have a look." Franzoni shined his flashlight above the control panel. It was hard to tell what was tucked up there with all the conduits in the way. With his light unsuccessfully penetrating the dark space, he asked Sauer to grab him something to stand on.

The young man returned with a small wooden crate. Franzoni stood on it and spread the conduits apart. "The kid's right. There's a black bag up here." He glanced at Witkowski, a look of fear in his eyes. "And there shouldn't be."

* * *

Witkowski left Sauer to watch over the first bag in the reefer room with strict instructions not to touch it and to keep everyone else out. The police officer and Franzoni rushed to the aft motor room (B-4), the location of the third X on the diagram.

They swept the room, convinced that if there was something amiss it would be in the form of the same type of bag. It didn't take long before Franzoni called out that he'd found another one stuffed behind the propulsion motor. Witkowski rushed Franzoni out of the room and back toward the reefer room where they picked up a very nervous Danny Sauer. The three men hustled out of the *Slater*'s lower spaces and back into the bright morning sunshine.

* * *

The area around the USS *Slater* erupted into organized chaos moments after Witkowski, Franzoni, and Sauer burst onto the deck of the old warship. They bounded across the gangway and onto the dock as fast as their feet could take them. An out-of-breath Witkowski called the situation in while Flynn worked with Franzoni to verify all crew members were off the *Slater*. Patrol cars from around the city came screeching into the small parking lot near the warship's dock. Police officers quickly set up barricades and closed off nearby Quay Street and the Dunn Memorial Bridge, and buildings in close proximity were evacuated. Albany Fire Department vehicles arrived at the dock while their rescue boat closed off all river traffic around the USS *Slater*. The New York State Police Bomb Disposal Unit (BDU) arrived and began preparations to board the warship. Last to arrive were numerous news vans, setting up as close as they could so as not to miss any of the action.

Chapter Twenty-One
Albany, NY
July 2, 9:03 AM

Andy Kohler sat behind his desk facing Kyle Fitzpatrick and me. The only sound was the angry drumming of his fingertips on the desktop. He had not expected to see us this morning, but when we showed up refusing to be turned away, he decided to hear us out. Especially after I leaned toward him in the busy hallway and quietly threatened to alert the news media that he was using us to help him step on the demonstrators' civil rights. Kohler was quick to point out that Kyle and I knew that was not the truth, but he also understood that once the dogs in the media got that bone in their mouths they wouldn't let it go. He grudgingly led us into his office, instructing his administrative assistant not to disturb him.

"I explained before we began that I have to watch from the shadows on this," Kohler said. "For you to try to blackmail me is—"

"Here's something you weren't aware of," I said, cutting him off. "We believe this Gregory guy kidnapped

Kyle's sister, Megan, and is holding her."

Kohler rocketed from his seat, the plush swivel chair rolling backward and smacking the paneled wall behind him. "What have you gotten me into?" He stepped from behind his desk, keeping a hand on its polished surface to steady himself.

"There wasn't any point in telling you about Megan at the time," I explained. "Our plan was to use your office to help us find this guy. We'd get Megan back and you'd get your audience with the leader of the group that's driving you crazy."

"When someone is kidnapped," said Kohler, "common sense says the perpetrators want a ransom of some kind." He rubbed his throbbing forehead. "And you call yourself a private investigator." He shuffled over to the large window overlooking West Capitol Park. "What in God's name have I gotten myself into?"

Now Kyle spoke. "Look, I'm trying to save my sister's life. We thought you could help, but I guess you're only concerned with your own ass. And that of your handler, Governor Clifton."

Kohler spun around to face Kyle. "You listen to me, you sonofabitch. You came to me. Remember? I only wanted to speak with the person in charge of the group harassing the governor. Just talk. That was all." He paused to catch his breath. "Now you tell me he could be a maniac and may have kidnapped your sister? That's what you've gotten me tangled up with? Why didn't you just go to the police for help? Or the FBI?"

Kyle walked toward Kohler, the press secretary inching backward, unsure of Fitzpatrick's intentions. "We were warned not to go to the authorities, that he had eyes in the Albany Police Department. For all we knew, he had eyes in the FBI too."

"We had to believe him," I said. "We couldn't take a chance with Megan's life." There was a moment of silence between the three of us. "What would you have done if it was *your* sister?" I noticed Kohler's worn wedding band. "Or your wife?"

Andy Kohler had made a living with words, always having them ready at a moment's notice no matter the situation. Now he stood silent.

There was a knock at the door. Enid Walker burst into the office. Kohler glanced at her, a look of surprise on his face. "Enid, I'm in the middle of—"

Walker moved quickly across the room to a large flat-screen television sitting on a credenza and snatched up the remote. "I'm sorry to barge in, Andy, but there's something you need to see right away." She turned the television on, tuning it to the local all-news channel. "I'm sure the governor is going to beat a path to your door as soon as she sees this, which will probably be any second now."

The screen came to life, displaying a young woman with blue eyes and shoulder length chestnut hair clutching a microphone. Large red letters announcing *breaking news* repeatedly crawled across the bottom of the screen. In the distance behind the reporter, Kohler could make out the USS *Slater* sitting serenely at its dock. He caught his breath when he saw that the entire area around the old warship was saturated with vehicles from the Albany Police Department, the Albany Fire Department, and the New York State Police, all of them with a multitude of colored lights flashing. "Jesus, now what..." he mumbled. Kyle and I joined him in front of the screen. Walker turned up the sound.

"It appears at least two explosive devices were found on the USS *Slater* this morning. As of yet, we do not know how they got there or who placed them aboard. The crew has been evacuated and the bridge and roads near the ship have been blocked off. The New York State Police Bomb Disposal Unit is preparing to board the vessel and examine the devices. This is a developing story so the only thing we know for sure is that two suspicious and potentially dangerous devices were found." The cameraman panned over and focused on the Albany Fire Department vessel blocking the river, then swung back to the reporter. "There is speculation that there may be a connection between the devices and an unidentified body found floating this morning near the *Slater*. That's all we have for now but we will continue to let you know as developments unfold. This is Connie Hernandez for—" Walker hit the mute button as the phone on Kohler's desk buzzed.

"And there's the boss now," Walker said, heading back to her office.

"Marco!" Kohler shouted. His administrative assistant, Marco Theopolis, stuck his head through the doorway. "Grab that and let the governor know I'm sorry but I can't speak right now. Tell her I am aware of the situation on the *Slater* and I will report to her within the next five minutes."

Kohler turned to Kyle and me. "This meeting is over."

"What about my sister?" Kyle asked. "What are we supposed to do now?"

"The governor is scheduled to announce her presidential campaign aboard the USS *Slater* on July 4th. Her announcement must happen there no matter what. That trumps your problem. I truly am sorry about your sister, but I must insist you leave immediately."

While Kohler and Kyle argued, something sparked

in my brain, something that was at best a million-to-one shot. I tuned out the others and analyzed the two points my brain had connected with a very thin, almost non-existent, thread. I continued to watch the muted scene on the television screen, thinking of the possibility, trying to fit the pieces from these two different puzzles together. It was truly one of those rare moments in life when you suddenly and without explanation experience a split second of clarity, when things rise from the confusing quagmire enveloping you and make complete sense.

"Wait!" I said, louder than I had intended. Kohler and Kyle stopped talking. "Kyle, how did Gregory describe what he wanted to do? Tell me exactly what he said to you, word for word."

"He never got into specific details," Kyle said. "He told me he had the perfect plan to topple Governor Clifton once and for all, that it would be an explosive statement."

I tapped my finger against the television screen. "This is it. This is what he's planning to do. An explosive end to Governor Clifton. Explosive. And on July 4th. The same day he promised to release Kyle's sister if we kept quiet about him. This was never about a cash ransom. It was about guaranteeing Kyle kept his mouth shut. Now is it time to get seriously involved?"

Kohler folded his arms across his chest. "Do you expect me to believe that some radical nut job leading a pack of screaming hyenas in the park planted bombs aboard the *Slater* in an attempt to kill the governor of New York State? Do you realize how absurd that sounds?"

Kyle joined the fray. "Jesus, Rick. It makes sense."

"And what of the dead body found there this morning?" Kohler said. "I suppose that figures into your little conspiracy theory also?"

"That person could have been connected," I said. "Look, I don't have all the answers. Not yet, anyway. But there's just too much circumstantial evidence here not to investigate it."

"I think you're reading way too much into this purely out of desperation," Kohler said.

I knew my time had run out. I yanked the picture of Gregory out of my shirt pocket and slapped it on Kohler's desk. "This is Gregory's picture. We found it ourselves from the news footage shot around the park. Please, just check it out. You have plenty of resources to make this happen." Kohler remained silent. "And look at the footage shot at the port the night the *Slater* arrived. See if this guy is in the crowd. That will prove what we're saying."

"I spoke with this guy a couple of times," Kyle said. "I'm telling you, if he tried to kill your boss once, I guarantee he'll try it again." He stepped in toward Kohler. "If he launches another attack on the governor, I promise you that I will be the first one to tell the story of how it came to be. And I will tell the story as loud as I can."

Kohler opened the door, dismissing us, the two men who were trying desperately to save Megan Fitzpatrick's life. "Go. Now." Kyle and I stood rooted in place. "I promise to call you back in an hour. I have to speak with the local authorities and the governor right now." Still no movement from us. "One hour. I promise." Kyle passed slowly through the doorway. I lingered a moment before addressing Kohler in a somber tone.

"We're not going to blackmail you. We just want to get Kyle's sister back. Please." Kohler nodded as I rushed to catch up to Kyle.

Chapter Twenty-Two
Schenectady, NY
July 2, 10:41 AM

"No, no, no!" Gregory Rockwell screamed. His outburst was answered by the sound of someone in the room next door banging on the wall, followed by a male voice spewing a string of drunken obscenities, threatening him if he didn't shut the hell up. Rockwell ignored the degenerate living on the other side of the wall. He glared at the breaking news report on the television screen showing his grand scheme to destroy Governor Helen Clifton crumbling right before his eyes.

He dropped his head in his hands, on the verge of tears, as he struggled with what to do next. It was a simple plan, foolproof even, but now it was all over. How had they found the bombs? They were supposed to be hidden in out-of-the-way places where no one would ever look. That sonofabitch Anson must have failed to place them exactly where he had told him to. He held no regret for killing the bastard now.

He tried to focus on the reporter speaking. Something she had said nagged at him, but he couldn't put his finger on it.

"It appears at least two explosive devices were found on the USS *Slater* this morning. As of yet, we do not know how they got there or who placed them aboard. The crew has been evacuated and the bridge and roads near the ship have been blocked off. The New York State Police Bomb Disposal Unit is preparing to board the vessel and examine the devices. This is a developing story so the only thing we know for sure is that two suspicious, and potentially dangerous, devices were found." The female reporter's face was replaced by a large ship with the Albany Fire Department name emblazoned on its side. The vessel seemed to be blocking the river. The picture changed again, displaying the young female reporter. "There is speculation that there may be a connection between the devices and the unidentified body that was found floating this morning near the *Slater*. That's all we have for now but we will continue to let you know as developments unfold. This is Connie Hernandez for—"

Two devices? She said two devices! They had no idea there was a third bomb still in play. Rockwell snatched his cell phone off a nightstand that had seen better days and pressed the number for Phil Crowley.

"Yeah," Crowley mumbled.

"Have you seen today's news?"

"Looking at it now," he said. "I'm guessing this changes things."

"I need you to pick me up right away. We're going to the barn," Rockwell said. "It's time we spoke about your drone."

"Gladly. Be there in twenty minutes."

Rockwell then called Tony Zacarelli, ordering him to keep an eye on the demonstrators at West Capitol Park to make sure they were as noisy and disruptive as they could be. He also warned him to be careful not to get spotted by Patterson and Fitzpatrick should they appear. He went back to watching the news. There was still a chance he could crush Helen Clifton, but only one. He had to make it count.

Chapter Twenty-Three
Abandoned farm
Thirteen miles southeast of Albany, NY
July 2, 11:26 AM

Phil Crowley checked the rear-view mirror, then jerked the wheel to the left. The brown hatchback abruptly left the road and lunged for a well-concealed dirt path that led into the woods. Branches from encroaching trees and bushes rubbed against the sides of the vehicle producing a symphony of scratching sounds. The car eventually emerged into a clearing near the barn housing Megan Fitzpatrick. Crowley pulled behind the structure and killed the engine. He and Gregory Rockwell sat for a long moment with the windows rolled down, listening to make sure they had not been followed.

"Do you really think your drone can do it?" said Rockwell. "The crowd is going to be huge. People are going to see it."

"Got it all figured out." Crowley twisted around and angled his arm into the floor space behind the passenger seat. A few grunts later he came up with a small plastic bag from a local dollar store. He placed it on the console between the front seats and pulled out a roll of blue streamers. Digging into the bag, he came up with two more rolls, one red and one white. "I'm going to attach these streamers to the drone and circle the ship. Make it look all kinds of patriotic. The law enforcement guys will think Clifton's people put on the display and just forgot to clear it with them. By the time they find out it's not theirs, it'll be too late."

"And how can you be so sure they won't shoot the thing down?"

Crowley's hand disappeared into the bag. He pulled out one last roll of material. "Not with it pulling this," he said. "In fact, I'm betting Clifton's people will be crawling over each other to take credit for this little stunt when they see it flying overhead." Crowley unrolled a white banner that read *Clifton for President* in large blue letters. Rockwell shook his head, amazed at the simplicity of Crowley's plan. "I know. Pure genius, right?"

"Is it safe to test it around here?" Rockwell said.

"It's actually pretty quiet. Help me get it out of the trunk and I'll fire it up." Crowley paused. "What about your friend inside?" He nodded toward the barn. "She's quiet now but she might start yelling again if she realizes we're out here."

"Let her scream. I have more important things to worry about."

The two men climbed out of the vehicle. Crowley opened the rear hatch and pulled aside an old wool blanket stretched across the cargo area. There lay something straight out of a science-fiction movie; it was painted a flat black and looked like a crab on steroids.

"Pretty wild, huh?" Crowley noted the look of surprise on Rockwell's face. "It started out as a standard quadcopter. I added four more motors and amped up the power source. This thing has some balls now with eight motors on it. It can easily haul our last bomb once I repackage it in this." He lifted what appeared to be an oversized rectangular shoebox out of the cargo area and handed it to Rockwell. The box was made of cardboard and covered in red and white stripes.

"How long can it stay up?" Rockwell asked.

"We'll be fine. We don't need a lot of linger time," Crowley said. "We circle the ship a few times just for laughs, then swoop in and kamikaze Clifton's ass."

"And the maximum range on this?"

"That won't be a problem," Crowley said. "We'll borrow the white van again and launch the drone from a vacant building I already scoped out in Albany's South End. We'll be well within range. And we don't have to be able to physically see the *Slater* to deliver our package." He pointed to a tiny box on the front of the drone. "This camera will be our eyes."

"There are going to be a lot of other eyes on it," Rockwell said. "The entire area will be crawling with law enforcement."

"So we need to figure out some way to thin the herd," Crowley said. They lifted the drone out of the trunk and placed it on the ground behind the vehicle. Crowley then retrieved the control unit and began powering it up.

While Crowley was preparing the drone for its test flight, Rockwell was thinking of a way to draw attention away from it as it swooped in on the *Slater*. "I may have an idea," he said. Crowley stopped his tinkering long enough to listen. "We plant dummy pipe bombs all around the city just as the festivities begin."

Crowley nodded, obviously seeing the possibilities. "They'll have to cut loose part of the force guarding the

Slater to run all around Albany, trying to figure out if they're under a legitimate explosive attack. It could move enough of them away from the ship."

Rockwell slipped his cell phone out of his jeans pocket. "I'll call Tony and let him know." He checked his wristwatch. "He can meet us here after today's demonstration at the Capitol is over. In the meantime, you and I will pick up everything we need. The three of us will get the packages put together before the night is over, then decide on a timetable and destinations."

"Sounds like a plan, boss." Crowley turned on the control unit. "Ready for a test flight?"

Crowley activated the drone's eight small motors. The buzz wasn't as loud as Rockwell had feared, but it was still noticeable. The controller resembled a simple tablet. There were multiple windows on it showing the view from the camera along with battery status, motor vitals, altitude, speed, and direction. A set of joysticks bracketed the display.

Crowley increased power to the motors and the drone gently lifted off the ground, coming to a hover twenty feet above their heads. "Figure the barn is the *Slater*." Keeping his eyes on the drone, he increased altitude slightly and sent the drone off. It came to a stop approximately 300 feet away. Rockwell watched the image being sent back to the controller's screen from the onboard camera. He could see the barn and himself next to Crowley.

"Here's what I'm thinking," Crowley said as the drone moved slowly toward the barn. "A nice slow, non-threatening approach." The drone circled the barn. "Followed by a loop around the ship to get everyone's attention, and then..." At the front of the barn the drone stopped and darted forward. Just before it slammed into the structure, Crowley sent it rocketing upward, just missing the peak of the sagging roof. He brought it back around and landed it softly at their feet. He shut down the motors and quiet once again took over. "We bury this thing right at the governor's feet. End of story."

"That was perfect," Rockwell said. *End of a long, terrible story of Helen Clifton being a political cutthroat.* "Let's pack up and get going. We have a long night ahead of us."

* * *

Megan Fitzpatrick thought she heard bees. Dozens, maybe hundreds. And they sounded angry. She managed to pry one of her sleep-encrusted eyes open, then slammed it shut again. It wasn't a dream. She really was lying on the dirt floor of a barn. Still.

The young captive lifted her head and squinted in the light coming through the gaps in the walls. *How long have I been here? Two days? No. Three days. I think.* She yanked at the chain connected to the leather restraint on her right ankle, then pounded the ground in frustration with her fist. Megan stopped her assault on the dirt floor and curled up under the coarse wool blanket, resting her head on her arms. She was still tethered to the unyielding chain attached to the post supporting the roof, and unless she figured a way to get it off, she wasn't going anywhere.

What is that constant buzzing noise outside? She pushed her face further into her arms to escape the sound when suddenly something stung her cheek. Megan lifted her head and saw the culprit; she had been pricked by the brooch attached to the lapel of her blazer. She gazed at the brooch. It was nothing more than a delicate ring of bright silver about an inch and three-quarters in diameter. The inside of it contained a silver palm tree with green leaves made of some shiny stones. There was also a colorful toucan, decorated with stones of blue, red, and yellow.

Staring at the brooch brought a smile to her face. It had been a gift from Rick Patterson, her boyfriend at the time. They were on a cruise in the Cayman Islands when she saw it in a small shop and mentioned how pretty it was. Megan never knew he had gone back to the shop while she was busy taking photographs of the beautiful Caribbean scenery. Rick surprised her with it at dinner that night.

Megan unclipped the brooch and held it up. A shaft of sunlight struck it, making the colored stones come alive. She recalled that vacation as one of the best times of her life, and one of her last with Rick. They had seemed perfect for each other, but that shooting accident when he was a police officer changed him. He became moody and short-tempered. She tried to help him get through the pain of losing his partner but she was unable to reach him across the cold, wide chasm that divided them. She still thought of Rick Patterson often, sometimes reaching for the phone to call him, but never having the courage to dial.

Megan wondered what made her grab the brooch that morning and put it on. It was truly an unconscious, last-minute move as she was heading out the door. She glanced at the brooch one more time, intending to put it in her pocket. She froze, examining the back. It had a long pin about an inch and three-quarters long which secured it to her blazer. She shoved the tattered blanket away.

Megan flicked the pin open, then curled her legs up and examined the leather cuff on her ankle. It was a simple leather cuff with a sheepskin lining, similar to a hospital restraint. There was a small lock that kept it tight enough so she could not slip her ankle through. Another small lock connected the chain to a metal loop. *And of course the chain connects me to the entire damn barn.*

Megan took the point of the pin and began to poke and prod at the stitching on the cuff. Being cautious not to bend the pin, she finally wedged its dull point under the thread, twisting it back and forth. The tough thread began to stretch. A few tense minutes later it finally broke. She glanced toward the door, listened intently. The buzzing sound had ceased. Confident she was all alone, she attacked the rest of the stitching on the cuff. There was a lot of stitching yet to go before she would find out if her efforts would be rewarded. But Megan Fitzpatrick finally had a plan to free herself.

Chapter Twenty-Four
Albany, NY
July 2, 11:51 AM

The NYS State Capitol Building was a madhouse. The hallways were packed with uniformed men and women rushing from office to office, weaving around legislators and staffers.

Kyle Fitzpatrick and I loitered at the foot of the building's Great Western Staircase, better known as the Million Dollar Staircase, as people rushed up and down the stairs. I glanced at my watch. The one-hour time limit Andy Kohler had promised us had slipped by. We had no alternative but to wait amidst thc maclstrom until Kohler summoned us back.

Kyle nudged me with his elbow, then nodded up the grand staircase. Kohler stood on the landing above us flanked by a pair of New York State Troopers. He waved us up.

"Show time," I said. We charged up the stairs two steps at a time. Without a word, Kohler motioned for us to follow him. We fell in behind Kohler, the two troopers bringing up the rear. The crowds in the hallways moved aside before Kohler, like Moses parting the Red Sea. Kohler's entourage proceeded through the maze of hallways, finally entering a meeting room.

I halted abruptly in the doorway, Kyle almost colliding with me from behind. I scanned the room, astounded at the scene before me. Men and women in a wide array of law enforcement garb sat around the longest table I had ever seen. Even more personnel stood against the walls. It became eerily quiet when they saw Kohler.

"Here," Kohler said, pointing to a pair of empty chairs near the head of the table. Kyle pulled a chair out and sat.

I leaned into Kohler. "What did you get us into?"

"It's time to come clean," Kohler said loud enough for the entire room to hear. "Your dilemma has now become our dilemma." He pulled out the chair next to Kyle. "Sit."

I took in the crowd gathered around the table and along the walls. My eyes stopped on one of the attendees seated halfway down on the left side. *Just when I thought it couldn't get any worse.* There sat Albany Police Department Lieutenant Larry Dawson, one of my former superiors from my days on the APD. I had been *persona non grata* in Dawson's eyes since the shooting that took the life of my partner, Sergeant Dave Taylor. It could have been my imagination, but it seemed to me as if Dawson might be struggling to suppress a scowl.

"May I have your attention, please," Kohler said. The room went completely silent, all eyes on him, all eyes except Dawson's, which were locked on me. "Governor Clifton extends her appreciation to members of the Albany Police Department, the Albany Fire Department, the New York State Troopers, and representatives of the

FBI and Homeland Security for their prompt response to the situation aboard the USS *Slater*." He nodded toward Kyle and me. "This is Rick Patterson, a private investigator, and Kyle Fitzpatrick, a freelance writer, both locals. They have critical information which may assist us in locating the person or persons responsible for planting the explosive devices on the ship."

An eighty-inch flat-screen television hung from one of the paneled walls. The screen was split into six separate sections, each one displaying a different view of the area surrounding the USS *Slater*. Kohler motioned toward the muted screen. "These images are being fed to us in real-time by a number of cameras set up by the Albany Police Department." Kohler paused as the entire room stared at the action on the screen. Two figures clad head-to-toe in bulky olive-drab bomb suits shuffled off the ship carrying a black rucksack. "Can someone tell us what's happening right now?"

One of the New York State Troopers shot to his feet. "The New York State Police Bomb Disposal Unit has deactivated the first of the two devices. It is now being removed from the ship and will be placed in a disposal trailer to be taken away. They will execute the same procedure on the second device. We hope to know more once the devices are dismantled and checked for prints."

"Anyone else?" Kohler said.

A young woman in a navy-blue pant suit and white blouse stood. "I'm FBI Agent Susan Kazakova. This concerns Carter Anson, a welder assigned to perform repair work on the USS *Slater*, found dead this morning in the Hudson River in the vicinity of the vessel. An FBI team is currently combing through Anson's apartment in Brooklyn. A second team is processing a late model black

Ford F-150 believed to be his vehicle located in the Caddell Dry Dock parking lot, where the *Slater* had been docked until recently, undergoing repairs. We're checking to see if there is any evidence connecting him to the devices found on the *Slater*. His death may simply be an accident. We're waiting for the medical examiner's findings."

"Anyone else before I explain about Patterson and Fitzpatrick's presence at this meeting?"

A burly, middle-aged man in a black suit stood. "Frank Genovese, Homeland Security. One of our teams is currently examining all news footage shot the night the *Slater* arrived in Albany. A bulletin has been put out asking the public for any videos they may have taken that night." Kohler's administrative assistant, Marco Theopolis, thumbed the remote. A photograph appeared in the upper middle section of the screen. "This is a person of interest we are searching for." Kyle and I jerked upright as we stared at the photograph we had given to Kohler.

The representative from Homeland Security continued. "This man may be connected to the explosive devices. He goes by the name of Gregory, last name unknown at this time, and he is said to be the head of one of the groups demonstrating most vocally against Governor Clifton. Mr. Kohler put this photograph in our hands and asked us to get started while he promised more information to follow."

"I am going to let you hear from Rick Patterson and Kyle Fitzpatrick regarding their involvement," said Kohler. "I believe they may be able to fill in some of the gaps in your investigation."

Kyle sat, almost in a trance. I laid my hand on his shoulder. "Easy, Kyle," I said softly. "We have to give them everything. It's time."

"I just killed my sister," Kyle groaned. "We weren't supposed to say anything. Not a word to anyone. And now everyone in this room knows. I failed her."

I turned to face the room. "Kyle Fitzpatrick came to me on June 30th. He told me a story I had trouble believing but I stuck with him because I've known him a long time. And in all that time his word has always been good. I also know his sister, Megan, and I will save her, with or without your help."

I launched into a twenty-minute dissertation detailing everything we had done and discovered over the past three days in our search for Gregory. Kyle interjected a few comments at key moments. "And that's what we've got," I concluded.

"And it took you three days to report this kidnapping?" Susan Kazakova said. "That's seventy-two hours we could have used to catch this guy. Seventy-two very valuable hours that we can't get back."

Kyle shot to his feet, stabbing a finger at Gregory's frozen image on the screen. "This bastard told us he had eyes in the Albany Police Department. That he would know if we reached out for help. Were we supposed to gamble with my sister's life and just assume he was a liar?"

Lieutenant Larry Dawson now jumped up. "Don't you dare make accusations that officers under my command are working with this person. And furthermore, how can you be so damn sure this is the person who's even involved?"

"All I'm saying is what he told me," Kyle said. "I spoke with him. Hell, I met him face to face. He's involved right up to his eyeballs, and I know he's got my sister."

I nudged Kyle back down into his seat. "Look, we

did the best we could. Megan Fitzpatrick's abduction wasn't a typical kidnapping. They weren't looking for ransom. They promised to let her go, even giving us the time and place to pick her up. All they wanted was our silence until July 4th."

I waited for some reaction. None. "Can't you see the connection between this Gregory guy, the governor's appearance on the *Slater* on July 4th, and the bombs being placed on the ship? It's got to be why he wanted Kyle silenced. Even if Kyle didn't know the specifics, he might have figured out enough to blow Gregory's plan to hell." I had given these people everything we had. It was up to them to decide if they would run with the ball. "Are you going to help us? Because if you're not, Kyle and I are out of here, right now. We'll find Megan on our own."

Kohler took control of the meeting. "That's why they're all here. In fact, some of these agencies are already working on this case."

"That's correct," Susan Kazakova said. "If we can tie the deceased *Slater* crewmember to Gregory, it could shine a light on new leads."

"And we're running Gregory's face through every database known to man," Frank Genovese added. "I'm confident we'll have a name very soon."

"My biggest concern is the governor's appearance aboard the *Slater* on July 4th," said Kohler. "It will be the biggest announcement of her political career. It has to happen on that day, and she is adamant that it happen on that ship." Kohler scanned the room. "But how safe is it? How wise?"

"We have sealed off the entire area around the ship," Dawson said. "It's a hell of a lot safer than it was this morning. If we're starting with a clean slate right now we can regulate everything and everyone entering that area."

"So you're saying what, exactly?"

"I'm saying that as long as we keep the area locked down from this moment on, the governor will be safe," Dawson said. "I have personnel crawling all over that dock and the surrounding area right now and I have no plans on moving them, so if that's where the governor wants to have her big day, I say she should."

Kohler looked around the table. "What's the opinion of the rest of you?" One by one, the other agencies all fell in line behind Dawson. "Okay. I will pass the news on to Governor Clifton. I want hourly updates from this point forward until proceedings aboard the *Slater* have concluded." Kohler addressed Kyle and me. "I have your cell numbers if we find out anything new."

With Kohler gone, I stood and called out loud enough to stop everyone in their tracks. "And what about Megan Fitzpatrick? I'm not hearing anything about her."

Lieutenant Larry Dawson spoke up. "As soon as we learn more about this person of interest from the FBI and Homeland Security, we'll be in a better position to move forward. We find him, we find the kidnapping victim, and just maybe stop a bomb from going off. Until then," he said, "stay out of the professionals' way." He brushed past me without a word.

Dawson's actions didn't shock me in the least. He had been at war with me since Dave Taylor's death. I had no reason to believe Dawson's attitude would ever change.

"C'mon, Kyle," I said. "We've got work to do. We're not trusting Megan's life to these people. They're more concerned with the governor and her big announcement." We joined the stream of attendees exiting the meeting room, then strode down the Million Dollar Staircase and exited the building.

Chapter Twenty-Five
Albany, NY
July 2, 1:38 PM

Tony Zacarelli sat on a bench in West Capitol Park enjoying a cold can of Coke while he watched Rockwell's faction demonstrate just outside the Capitol building. He was positive Governor Clifton couldn't hear their raucous chants from inside her stout fortress. In spite of that, they seemed happy enough marching around with their little placards and yelling nonsensical rhymes.

Rockwell had called earlier to tell him to stop at the barn after nightfall.

Zacarelli checked his watch again. Another hour or so and he would send Rockwell's demonstrators packing for the day. He was looking forward to this whole thing being over. All he wanted at this point was to get the rest of his money from Rockwell and blow this town; he was way overdue to get back on the road to places unknown. Tossing his empty soda can to the ground, he headed for the crowd. Time to check on the flock.

* * *

Since leaving Kohler's meeting, Kyle and I had

walked around the park searching for the elusive Gregory. I believed more than ever that Gregory had to pop out of his hole soon, especially if he was planning something big in only two more days.

I wandered the State Street side of the park while Kyle roamed the Washington Avenue side. I stopped to pick Kyle out of the crowd. I watched him systematically stop everyone he came across and flash Gregory's photograph before moving on. Just as I was about to resume my own patrol, Kyle took off like a rocket, ramming into the swarm of Gregory's followers. *What the hell?* A man darted between a pair of food vendors right into the heavy midday traffic on Washington Avenue. Horns blared and tires screeched as he tore across the four-lane street and ran toward the sprawling New York State Education Department building, Kyle hot on his heels. I took off, trying desperately to catch up.

The man raced up Washington Avenue, then cut right onto South Swan Street, Kyle still on his tail but unable to close the distance. At the end of South Swan Street, the guy darted through skidding traffic to get across Elk Street, sped through a crowded parking lot, and disappeared into the bordering neighborhood.

I caught up to Kyle at the edge of the parking lot. He was doubled over, trying to catch his breath. "You okay?"

"Gimme a second," Kyle said.

"Who the hell was that?"

"It was that guy I pinned against the wall for following me yesterday. Sonofabitch runs like a damn gazelle."

"You're sure it was the same guy?"

"Positive. Jeans, black jacket, red ball cap. Same ugly face."

"So what happened?"

"I saw him give orders to Gregory's demonstrators. He saw me and bolted. I knew this sonofabitch was dirty when I grabbed him yesterday. He wasn't waiting for a goddamn bus. He was following me." Kyle closed his eyes. "He's *got* to be tied in with Gregory."

"I never got a good look at him so I can't say if he was the same guy," I said. "But I believe you, Kyle."

Kyle yanked his cell phone from his pocket. "You don't have to believe me. Check it for yourself."

I examined the image on Kyle's phone. "I'll be damned. Same guy, all right." I forwarded the man's photograph to Kohler who vowed to get it to Homeland Security.

"Now we get to see if this guy is the break we've been looking for," I said. We headed back to Kohler's office, a little more optimistic than when we had left there. Along the way we came across Gregory's people and stopped to asked what they knew about the guy we had chased off. It came as no surprise that not one single person admitted knowing him. I was positive they were lying but powerless to beat the truth out of them, as tempting as it was.

Chapter Twenty-Six
Albany, NY
July 2, 3:02 PM

The photo that Kyle Fitzpatrick had taken of Tony Zacarelli flashed onto the wall-mounted display in the same meeting room Kohler's team had used earlier. Frank Genovese, the agent from Homeland Security, stood next to the screen. "This is Anthony Patrick Zacarelli, male, 34. His last known address is a boarding house in Lexington, Kentucky. Unfortunately, his last known address is now an empty field where a boarding house used to be until it burned to the ground almost three years ago. Suffice it to say, Mr. Zacarelli has been off the radar for a while." A new image, a mug shot of Tony Zacarelli, flashed onto the screen. "He has an extensive list of priors throughout a good portion of the southeastern United States for various acts of theft, most of them petty. At this time it is unclear if he's connected to the explosive devices discovered on the USS *Slater* or the deceased crewman found this morning."

"Anything new on Gregory?" Kohler asked.

"We are treating him the same as Zacarelli—we have a BOLO out on him in addition to running his picture on electronic billboards and local television channels. Nothing yet."

"Well, this guy is involved," I said. "He was tailing Kyle yesterday, and when he saw Kyle approach him today, he took off like a scared rabbit. He's tied to Gregory, and by association, to the bombs. I stake my reputation on it." Larry Dawson emitted a soft snicker, just loud enough for me to hear.

Susan Kazakova, the FBI agent spoke up. "We've got our people morphing this Gregory's photo, things like removing his beard and adjusting his hair, to see if a younger or cleaned up version of him jogs anyone's memory."

"Contact my office immediately if you discover anything new," Kohler said. "In the meantime, this room will be our command center." He left to update Governor Clifton, hard at work in her office on the most important speech of her life. The rest of the attendees filed out to tackle their own tasks.

* * *

One person lingered, trying to kill time without looking obvious. He eventually became the last person in the meeting room. The man checked the hallway, then backed into the room, closing the door softly. He slipped a cell phone from his pocket and dialed a number. Eyes riveted to the meeting room door, he waited for the call to connect.

"Yeah?" a voice said.

"You have a problem." Silence. "Your man screwed up. Big time."

"How so?"

"He was spotted by the girl's brother. And the private investigator."

"How sure are they that it was him?"

"Pretty damn sure since they chased him for a couple of blocks before he gave them the slip. They took a photo of him and handed it over to the FBI, Homeland Security, the State Police, and the APD. They've put BOLOs out on both of you. And if you pass an electronic billboard or watch the local news, you'll see both your faces."

"They don't have enough time to stop us."

"Don't be so sure."

"Can you slow them down?"

"That wasn't part of the deal. I said I would be your inside man and that was all. I'm just giving you a heads-up to stay out of sight. I'll keep you updated if I can, but don't call me. I'll call you if I have anything." He disconnected, then slipped out of the room.

* * *

"Sonofabitch!" Rockwell's fist came crashing down on the dashboard. Phil Crowley jerked the steering wheel and the car nearly swerved into oncoming traffic.

"What happened?" said Crowley.

"We have to get off the streets. They're looking for me. And Zacarelli too." Rockwell and Crowley had just picked up supplies at an out of the way hardware store in Albany's South End. "We'll have to make due with what we've got."

"You're the boss."

"Let's get out to the barn." Rockwell glanced at his watch. "Can you get us there on the back roads?"

"As long as you point me toward them. After all, this is your town. I'm just passing through."

"Right." Rockwell gave Crowley directions, then pulled his cell phone from his pocket. He ordered Zacarelli to get out to the barn right away. "I won't tolerate another screw-up."

Chapter Twenty-Seven
Abandoned farm
Thirteen miles southeast of Albany, NY
July 2, 6:41 PM

Megan Fitzpatrick couldn't recall how long she had been here, silently chastising herself for not scratching off the days on the beam she was chained to. Her best guess was that she had been imprisoned in the same malodorous clothes for three days. But she couldn't be sure. Why had no one found her? Was anyone even aware she was missing?

Megan opened her clenched fist. Her eyes lingered upon her brooch. *Why I am holding this?* She suddenly remembered using the pin on the back of the brooch to rip the stitching on the cuff wrapped around her ankle.

She examined the cuff. Even though she had dug at the stitching with the dull point of the pin for what seemed an eternity, most of it was still intact. The cuff did not feel any looser than when she had started. With new resolve, Megan began to pick and pull at the stitching. The young captive refused to spend a fourth day chained up like an animal.

* * *

It took almost two hours but Megan finally broke the last of the stitching on the restraint. Still, the cuff refused to yield. She leaned back against the roof support. Sweat ran from her forehead, stinging her eyes. Wiping her sleeve along her brow, she examined the cuff in the dwindling light. It was still too snug to squeeze her foot through. She pushed and pulled at the lining. It was beginning to loosen. She gave it one last, strong push with her aching fingers. The lining slipped out and fell to the dirt floor.

She could hardly believe she had gotten this far. She pulled off her shoe and eased the cuff down her ankle, working it over her heel with great difficulty. It was snug, very snug, but suddenly, it slipped right over her arch and toes.

Megan used the roof support to help her get to her feet. She slipped her shoe back on. She honestly hadn't planned this far ahead. Moving to the workbench, she looked for her watch and cell phone, and found neither. There were some hand tools thrown haphazardly on the scarred wood surface, but nothing of use to her. Her eye caught the key that had to be to the lock on her cuff hanging from a nail above the workbench.

Moving to the doorway, she looked through the gap between the double doors, then pushed carefully. The doors eased opened an inch or two before the slack in the chain keeping them secured pulled tight. Megan's eyes swept the structure around her; no windows, and this was the only door leading out. It was beginning to get dark. She had to escape now while there was at least a little light.

Megan heard a low rumble, faint at first but growing louder. Soon it mixed with the sound of breaking branches. She peeked through the narrow gap between the doors. A small car pulled up to the front of the barn. She watched in silence as the vehicle came to a stop. A man climbed out and moved toward the doors.

She was about to scream for help when a beeping erupted from the man's pocket. He yanked a cell phone from the side pocket of his dirty jeans. She could only hear his half of the conversation but it became evident that he was not there to help her.

"Yeah?"

Silence.

"I just got here."

Silence.

"Hey, man, I got here as fast as I could but I had to stay off the main roads like you said."

Silence.

"Nah. I don't hear anything. She's quiet for once."

Silence.

"Right. See you when you get here." He lingered in front of the double doors and shook a cigarette from a crumpled pack. He lit it and inhaled deeply, savoring the smoke.

Megan backed away from the doors. Surprising this man when he entered would be her only chance at freedom. She made her way to the workbench. The broken handle of a shovel leaned against the wall. It was old, but solid, about four feet long. She hefted it in her hands, and swung it a few times like a batter getting ready to swing for the fence. Two strikes, three balls, last pitch. She would have one shot at this. He would come in any second now. She looked for the right place to hide.

Chapter Twenty-Eight
Abandoned farm
Thirteen miles southeast of Albany, NY
July 2, 8:57 PM

Tony Zacarelli checked his watch. He took one long, last drag from his cigarette, then dropped it to the ground, crushing it with his boot heel. Slipping a scrap of paper from his pocket, he dialed a series of numbers into the combination lock securing the rusty chain across the entrance. The lock sprang open. He snaked the chain out of the door handles and eased open one of the doors. It was dark inside. And quiet. He had forgotten to bring a flashlight. Fumbling with a Zippo lighter, he groped through the doorway. He found the lighter's thumbwheel and pushed.

* * *

Megan backed away from the door as it slowly swung open. She focused on the black silhouette of the man. A flame sprang from the shadows. The cigarette lighter illuminated the man's face. Megan reacted a fraction of a second before he did. The shovel handle connected with the side of his head. The lighter flickered out as the man collapsed to the floor. She slammed the shovel handle down where she heard him moaning. She stopped after a half dozen strikes.

Megan Fitzpatrick stood poised in the darkness, shovel handle ready to strike. Heavy breathing came from the floor in front of her. She dropped to her knees, her hands scrabbling around in the dirt. Her fingers brushed the Zippo lighter. She snatched it up and flicked the thumbwheel. Following the bright flame, she crept forward on her hands and knees. The man wasn't moving. His face was streaked with dark rivulets of blood. Most of her blows had landed on his head. She held her fingertips against his carotid artery. There was still a pulse.

Megan dashed to the workbench. She grabbed the key for the lock on the cuff and jammed it in her pocket, then rushed back to the man lying prone on the dirt floor. Her hands under his armpits, she dragged him with great effort to the chain attached to the roof support.

Placing the flaming lighter carefully on the floor, she turned the key and snapped the lock open. Megan yanked the man's boot off and tossed it into the darkness, then wrapped the leather cuff around his ankle. She tightened it as much as she could and put the lock back on. His moaning grew louder now as he struggled back to consciousness.

Megan rummaged through his pockets. No car keys. He must have left them in the ignition. She couldn't find his cell phone either. A vehicle approached through the foliage that surrounded the barn. Time for her to go. She shoved the lighter in her pocket, ran to the car and yanked the door open. The keys were in the ignition.

Before she could get into the car, the darkness enveloping her exploded in a blaze of bright light. A second vehicle pushed its way out of the foliage. Megan was pinned in the headlights. The vehicle accelerated toward her. It moved to block her in. Her only option was to abandon the car and run, using the night as a cloak to cover her escape.

Megan was no stranger to running, having been a standout on her high school track team. She kicked into high gear and crashed through a line of bushes, disappearing from the light. Shouting voices chased her from behind.

A loud crack shattered the night: once, twice, three times. She felt a white-hot strike from behind. Megan staggered a few steps before crashing to the ground. She tucked herself into a ball and rolled out of sight under the nearest bushes. Right before her mind shut down, Megan realized she had just been shot.

* * *

"What the hell are you doing?" Rockwell screamed. "I said no guns!"

"You think it's better to let her get away?" Crowley waved his weapon in Rockwell's face. "Your entire plan goes right down the crapper if she gets away."

"I told you, the only one who's going to die is Clifton."

"Maybe you should explain that to your buddy Carter Anson," Crowley said.

"No. More. Shooting." Rockwell clenched his jaw. "See where the hell Zacarelli is. I'll get the girl."

Crowley tucked the handgun into the back of his jeans. "Yeah, genius, you do that."

Crowley's flashlight swept from side to side in front of him. He proceeded carefully, ready to yank the handgun out of his waistband in spite of Rockwell's orders. The circle of light suddenly spilled over Zacarelli. Crowley froze. *You gotta be shitting me*, he thought.

Zacarelli was on his back on the dirt floor, unconscious, one boot off, the chain attached to the cuff locked on his ankle. "Sonofabitch," Crowley said. "Another genius." His hand rested on the grip of the handgun under his shirttail as he swept the flashlight beam around the rest of the barn checking for any more surprises.

Chapter Twenty-Nine
Albany, NY
July 2, 10:08 PM

The meeting room in the Capitol building buzzed with activity. Men and women sat at computers or milled around the room comparing notes and discussing strategies. The original attendees from earlier in the day had been replaced by fresh counterparts. Except for two: Kyle Fitzpatrick and me. Our vested interest in locating Gregory and Zacarelli kept us there no matter the time.

Maps of Albany sprouting pins with small colored flags were secured to the walls. Post-its adorned the outer edges. Information technology staff had installed two dozen computers lining the long conference table. The eighty-inch flat-screen television still displayed windows providing an array of video images from around the city.

I moved around the room, Styrofoam coffee cup in hand, observing the law enforcement personnel at work. Kyle was asleep in a swivel chair in a corner of the room, his head back, mouth open. I wished I could sleep. As much as I tried, my concern over finding Megan prevented me from drifting off. Rubbing the grit from my tired eyes, I raised the cup to my lips. I grimaced as I got a mouthful of cold, bitter coffee.

"We got us a name, people!" an FBI agent shouted as he kicked back from a computer screen and shot out of his seat. A hush fell over the room. "Meet Mr. Gregory Rockwell, one of the used-to-be rich New York Rockwells."

I jockeyed my way through the people gathered around the screen. A younger, cleaner, happier Gregory Rockwell appeared on the wall display sans hoodie and sunglasses. Soon after, a bio popped up next to his image.

"That's him!" Kyle was now fully awake. "That's the sonofabitch who's got my sister." He glared at Rockwell's image. "We got you, you bastard."

I maneuvered closer to the FBI agent. "How did you find him?" I asked.

"One of the images we morphed and put out to the public got a hit. Someone he went to college with. Said he was sure it was Gregory Rockwell. Once we got a name it was easy to find more. Turns out this guy's old man ran for governor and got his ass kicked by Helen Clifton."

"What happens now?"

"Not my call."

Kyle stood before the screen, arms folded, going through Rockwell's bio. I slid next to him and began reading. A graphic of a file folder containing news articles popped up on the screen. I tapped on the graphic and skimmed the articles.

It appeared the Rockwells had enjoyed a pretty good life until Gregory's father, Thomas, ran for governor. The old man started out doing well but the tide turned against him. He ended up getting crushed beneath the wheels of the Helen Clifton political machine. His business suffered major collateral damage. Thomas Rockwell lost everything, ended up in a mental institution, and died. It was rumored his wife, Suzanne, committed suicide. Gregory Rockwell dropped out of prestigious Rensselaer Polytechnic Institute in Troy, New York shortly after and disappeared. Until now. He was back with revenge on his mind and a debt to settle, a dangerous combination.

"I need some fresh air," I said. "If anything breaks come get me."

"Sure thing," Kyle said.

It would soon be midnight. Turning up the collar of my navy-blue jacket, I headed for a far corner of West Capitol Park. I was in search of a few minutes of peace to get my thoughts together. I had a feeling things were going to move pretty fast now.

* * *

Andy Kohler hurried into the room, struggling to get his suit jacket over his wrinkled white shirt. He tried in vain to straighten his red tie, finally giving up and yanking it off. He had been dozing on the leather couch in his office when a phone call from the FBI agent awakened him. He rushed to the images on the eighty-inch flat screen.

"Here's our man, sir," the FBI agent said.

Kohler studied Rockwell's image. "I remember this kid. He campaigned with his father against Governor Clifton." He scanned the news articles scrolling down the right side of the screen. "I remember these events all too well." Kohler scrutinized the obituaries for Rockwell's parents as they slid by. "Thomas and Suzanne Rockwell were decent people. Thomas Rockwell was just out of his league." *Well, Governor Clifton, your dirty politics may have just become a deadly boomerang,* he thought. "What happens now?"

"The appropriate agencies will use every resource to

locate Gregory Rockwell."

"Good," Kohler said. "Set up a meeting in two hours."

Andy Kohler would meet with Governor Helen Clifton first thing in the morning to fill her in on the bombs found on the USS *Slater*, Gregory Rockwell, and Tony Zacarelli. She had demanded timely updates and whenever those updates divulged nothing new the governor would tear into him. If history was any indication, he would continue to be her target for everything gone wrong.

* * *

The inside man slipped into the command center and circulated, soaking up as much information as he could. He froze when he saw Gregory Rockwell's face staring at him from the large wall screen. The inside man regained his composure, then casually drifted out of the command center. He made his way down the Million Dollar Staircase and left the Capitol building. He needed to find an isolated spot in the darkness of the empty park. He had another phone call to make.

* * *

The sky above West Capitol Park was peppered with pinpricks of brilliant light. I sat alone on a bench in the deserted park. The last three days had drained me, but I would not give up until I found Megan Fitzpatrick. *Maybe this is the universe giving me one more chance to make things right.*

I closed my weary eyes. The cool night air felt refreshing. *I just need five minutes of peace.* I was on the verge of nodding off when a soft *swish swish swish* caught my attention. Eyes still closed, I listened as it grew louder. It sounded like feet moving through the grass, getting closer.

I remained as still as the life-size bronze statue of

George Washington standing guard over the South Swan Street entrance to West Capitol Park. The *swish swish swish* stopped somewhere behind me. A subtle glance over my shoulder caught the dim glow from a cell phone screen. I didn't want to eavesdrop, but I had been there first and was just too damned tired to get up and move.

I could hear snippets of the caller's end of the conversation.

"It's me again."

Silence.

"They know who you are."

Silence.

"Someone (unintelligible) college identified you."

Silence.

"Don't blame (unintelligible). Your man screwed up things."

Silence.

"I already told you. I can't (unintelligible). Blame that idiot Zacarelli. I only agreed to be your eyes and ears on the inside."

My eyes shot open. *Did he say Zacarelli? Who the hell was this guy and who was he talking to?*

"You better keep your ass in the barn until (unintelligible) is over and then get the hell out of New York State."

Silence.

"That's not my problem. I don't give a (unintelligible) with the girl. Leave her there. She can't tell (unintelligible). And she can't implicate me in (unintelligible) kill the governor."

I shot off the bench, vaulted over it, and rushed toward the silhouette holding the phone. "Hey! You!" Before I could get a hand on him, the caller drove his fist into my stomach, dropping me to my knees. He threw a kick at my head, hitting me with a glancing blow that sent me to the ground, then took off like a world class sprinter.

Dazed, I lay on my side struggling to breathe. The shot to my gut had taken me completely by surprise. *Rookie mistake, Rick.* I rolled onto my back and watched as the stars winked out one by one.

* * *

"Rick! Come on, man, wake up."

I heard a faraway voice trying to push through the veil of fog surrounding me, then felt a gentle rocking, like I was back on that cruise ship in the Cayman Islands with Megan.

"Rick! For Christ's sake, wake up!"

My eyelids felt like lead. Kyle shined a flashlight in my face. I raised a hand to block the intrusive brightness. "Kyle? What happened?"

"What happened is right, Rick. When you didn't answer your cell I came out looking for you. What the hell happened?"

I struggled to sit up, finally making it with Kyle's help. Looking around me, I tried to collect my thoughts. My eyes swept across the bench I had been sitting on. "Help me up! Hurry!" Kyle hauled me to my unsteady feet. "I was dozing on that bench and a guy was right here, talking on his phone. He didn't see me but I heard him. I think he was talking to Gregory Rockwell."

"Hold on, Rick."

I grabbed Kyle by the front of his shirt and jerked him closer. "I know what I heard! I rushed him. He slugged me and took off. Wait! What time is it?"

Kyle checked his watch. "It's 11:10."

"Okay, so it's 11:10 right now. I came out here maybe 10:45. Five minutes to find this bench makes it

10:50. Another five minutes for his conversation and attacking me. That makes it 10:55." I thought a moment, still playing with the numbers.

"Hey, Rick, what say I get you up to Albany Medical Center and get your head looked at. Maybe you got hit harder than you think."

"Kyle, it's only been fifteen minutes since this happened. We have to find this guy."

"Okay, Rick. Say you're right and this mysterious stranger is involved. How do we find him?"

I tried desperately to recall the fragments of conversation I had heard. The cool night air was sharpening my mind. "He said they knew who he was. That someone from college knew him." I clenched my fists in desperation. "I'm not crazy, Kyle. I know what I heard."

"I believe you, Rick."

"He said something about a barn, and staying there until the heat was off. And that he didn't care what they did with the girl. It has to be Megan."

"Rick, why would this guy be out here in the dark talking about this? It doesn't make sense."

"I'll tell you why." I chose my words carefully. "This guy said he was only supposed to be Rockwell's eyes and ears on the inside."

"Are you saying—"

"This bastard has been in the meeting room with us the entire time."

Chapter Thirty
Abandoned farm
Thirteen miles southeast of Albany, NY
July 2, 11:19 PM

Rockwell stormed into the barn. He was very pissed off. Crowley had set up a few flashlights around the workbench. A soft moan came from Zacarelli slumped against the wall, one boot missing. His eyes were closed, face bloody, head drooping to the side.

"What the hell happened to him?" Rockwell said.

"Tough guy got his ass handed to him by your girlfriend," Crowley replied. "Speaking of which, where is she?"

"I couldn't find her," Rockwell said. "But I did come across a few splotches of blood. I hope all you did was wing her or else—"

"Or else what?" Crowley bristled. "Look around. I'm all you got left." Crowley grinned. "You're in no position to make threats."

Rockwell held up his cell phone. "I just got a call from my inside man. Not only have they identified Zacarelli, but now they know who I am too."

"Your plan is falling apart. Makes me think I should cut and run."

"You swore you were in this until the end," Rockwell said.

"I said I was in it for the money, and the money won't do me no good if I'm in prison. Or worse. So I'll ask again, what are you going to do about the girl?"

"She doesn't matter any more," Rockwell said. "We're way out here in the boonies and it looks like you wounded her. She doesn't pose a threat to us."

"You still haven't answered my question. Crowley glanced at Zacarelli as another moan slipped from the unconscious man's bloody mouth.

"Don't worry about the damn girl! We can still do this." Crowley was the only one who could pilot the drone. Without him, there was no drone, and without the drone, there was no paying Helen Clifton back for destroying his life. "We can assemble the dummy IEDs and be out of here in an hour. By the time the girl finds help, we'll be long gone."

Rockwell and Crowley spent the next forty-five minutes constructing dummy pipe bombs to distribute around the city of Albany. They worked diligently in silence, then loaded their harmless devices into the car. They lugged Zacarelli out of the barn and unceremoniously dumped him in the back seat. Crowley stashed Zacarelli's car inside the barn and chained the barn doors closed.

They intended to spend July 3rd hiding out in a place Crowley had found. There, they would get Zacarelli back on his feet and finalize plans for their July 4th assault.

With only one day left, Rockwell's plan was still alive, and Helen Clifton was still scheduled to die.

Chapter Thirty-One
Albany, NY
July 3, 12:11 AM

"And you're saying no one gets in or out of here without signing this log?" I stabbed my finger down on the ledger book.

"No one during the off-hours, from 6:00 PM until 6:00 AM, and all day on the weekends and holidays. And non-employees need a valid ID and someone to vouch for them," said the security guard at the front desk of the Capitol building. "No exceptions."

"We need to see the log from the time I signed out until right now," I said.

"Who are you looking for?" the guard asked.

"That's just it. We don't know," Kyle said as he reached for the ledger.

"We're not really supposed to let anyone see this log." The guard dropped his hand on the ledger to keep Kyle from turning it around. A second guard moved closer.

"How about I call Andy Kohler?" I said, trying hard not to have my suggestion sound like a threat.

The guard pointed to a phone on the desk. "Be my

guest."

I swung the phone toward me and dialed Kohler's extension. Someone answered on the first ring.

"Mr. Kohler's office." It was Marco Theopolis, Kohler's administrative assistant.

"This is Rick Patterson. I'm at the front security desk and I need to see the sign-in log. The guard on duty says he can't let me without authorization. I thought Andy Kohler could speak to him."

"I can check with him." Theopolis hesitated. "Can you tell me why you need to see the log?"

"I overheard a man speaking on his cell phone to someone I believe may be one of the men we're looking for. When I tried to grab him he slugged me and took off. I'm pretty sure he's someone who's been in the meetings with us."

"Do you know who you're looking for?"

"Not yet, but I think I can narrow it down if I check the sign-in log—" The line went dead. "Hello?" I shrugged. "I got disconnected." I dialed Kohler's extension again but the call went unanswered.

The guard tried calling Kohler's office. When no one answered, he turned to the other guard. "You want to check it out?"

The second guard was halfway up the staircase when the elevator doors near the security desk slid open. Marco Theopolis stuck his head out, a terrified look across his face. He sprinted toward the door leading out of the building.

"Hey! You! Get back here," the guard behind the desk shouted. "Stop that man!" The second guard hit the main floor and took off after Theopolis. The first guard snatched up his radio and alerted the rest of the security officers guarding the Capitol.

Unsure of what had just happened, Kyle and I exchanged glances, then tore after Theopolis.

* * *

Sal Campesi cranked up the radio. Drumming on the steering wheel, he checked the clock on the dashboard; it was just after midnight. He raced down State Street toward the Capitol with a huge order from his Uncle Bill's restaurant, *Billy B's Pizza Emporium.*

The tall stack of pizza boxes and Styrofoam containers let Campesi know there was something big going on at the Capitol tonight. Campesi's uncle had warned him that if he was late delivering an order this big, he would fire his ass. Sal Campesi pressed down harder on the gas pedal. The car rocketed through the intersection of State and South Swan Streets as the twenty-two-year-old delivery driver glanced once more at the dashboard clock.

* * *

Marco Theopolis was mesmerized by the changing images, reminding him of a child's kaleidoscope. First he saw the glowing streetlights, then the stars in the midnight sky, followed by the Capitol building. Then the scenes would repeat on a seemingly endless loop. And there was the sensation of floating on air. It all ended abruptly when his body exploded in pain and everything went dark.

* * *

Kyle and I skidded to a stop just outside the doors of the Capitol building. We watched in horror as a small car with a lit-up restaurant sign slammed into Marco Theopolis as he dashed across State Street. Theopolis somersaulted over the car's roof, his pinwheeling body crashing down onto the sidewalk along West Capitol Park.

The car jumped the curb and came to a screeching halt after narrowly missing a row of park benches. Four guards from the Capitol converged on the accident scene. One of the guards banged on the roof, yelling at the driver to shut the vehicle down and get out. The other three guards approached Theopolis. Two dropped down to check his condition as the third called for medical assistance.

Kyle and I ran across the street. Theopolis was in bad shape, his arms and legs twisted in unnatural positions. The delivery car driver sobbed. The sound of approaching sirens grew louder. We stood in silence, as the guards did what little they could.

"What the hell was that all about?" Kyle asked.

My eyes never left the critically-injured young man. "I think we've identified Rockwell's guy on the inside."

"But is he the only one?" Kyle said. "First it was just Rockwell, and then Zacarelli. Now this guy is involved too?" He shook his head in amazement. "Is there a whole conspiracy to kill Governor Clifton?"

"Why don't you go back inside and see if you can sneak a look at the sign-in log," I said.

* * *

A crowd of night staffers had gathered. Kyle weaved his way through the rubberneckers and made it back inside. The guard who had been manning the security desk had taken up station right inside the doors. When he saw Kyle enter the building, he turned back to his duty station.

"That's okay," Kyle said in his best I'm-your-buddy voice. "I know the procedure. I'll sign the log before going upstairs." The guard hesitated, then nodded. He knew Kyle and Rick were with Andy Kohler. He turned back to the accident scene. Kyle strode toward the security desk.

Kyle picked up a pen and spun the log around so it faced him. He ran his fingertip down the column containing names and found Patterson's.

"Got a problem?" It was the guard, facing him, hands on hips, looking very official.

"Uh, no," Kyle said. He raised the pen and shook it. "Trouble with the pen." The guard was still staring at him. If he didn't do something fast the guard would surely walk over to the security desk. Kyle reached under his jacket and yanked a pen out of his shirt pocket. "Got my own right here." He waved it in the air, then signed his name in the first empty slot along with the time. Kyle made a show of slipping the pen back in his shirt pocket, then nodded to the guard who turned his attention back to the accident scene.

Kyle discreetly eased his cell phone from his pants pocket and took a picture of the sign-in log. He couldn't chance using the flash. He slipped the phone back in his pocket and climbed the stairs to the meeting room to wait for Rick.

* * *

Twenty minutes later I strode into the second-floor meeting room and dropped into the seat next to Kyle. Most of the major players were back, summoned in the night via cell phone calls, text messages, and pagers. Kyle stared silently at me. I rubbed my tired eyes, looked at him, and shook my head. It was clear that Theopolis, the man we had chased into the street, had died, and with him any possible lead we had to finding Megan.

Kyle placed his phone on the conference table. "I got a shot of the security log," he said. "For all the good it does us now."

I picked up Kyle's phone and enlarged the picture of

the security log. Sure enough, the name right after mine was Marco Theopolis, Kohler's administrative assistant. Theopolis had signed in just before Kyle and I had reentered the building. He was the only person who had signed out and back in right after me, proof positive that Theopolis was the guy I had overheard on the phone in the park, and the guy who had sucker-punched me.

Andy Kohler entered the room. The man looked like he had aged one hundred years in the past few days. "Attention, please. Is there anything new on the search for Gregory Rockwell or Anthony Zacarelli?" There was no reaction from the crowd. He exhaled a long, deep breath. "We need to find these men as soon as possible. Governor Clifton refuses to change her plans. She fully intends to make her announcement from the USS *Slater* on July 4th and these two men are to be considered a viable threat.

"I have sad news. My administrative assistant, Marco Theopolis, was struck by an auto outside the building a short while ago. He has passed away." Kohler cleared his throat. "I'm sure you all noticed him in the background the last few days making sure our meetings ran smoothly." Kohler clasped his hands together. "If you would all join me in a prayer—"

"Before you make a saint out of this guy," I said, "I think you're going to want to hear what I have to say." Kohler looked stunned by the interruption.

I stood and addressed the room. "A short while ago I stepped outside for a breather. I found a deserted bench in West Capitol Park and sat there trying to get a few minutes of rest. Someone took up station near me in the dark. He was on a cell phone, unaware I was there. I heard enough of his conversation to convince me he was speaking with Gregory Rockwell or one of his people. I am certain that person was Marco Theopolis." I held my hands up to silence the questions. "Theopolis was an inside man for Gregory Rockwell."

"How can we be sure that's what you heard?" Kohler said. "Are you so certain that in your weary state of mind you heard things correctly?" Lieutenant Larry Dawson snickered.

"I was wide awake." Dawson opened his mouth to speak but I cut him off with a pointed finger. "Not a word, you pompous fool. If it wasn't for me and Kyle you would still be wandering around in the dark."

"Come on, Patterson," Dawson shouted. "You're grandstanding!"

I glared at Dawson. "I guarantee Theopolis was an inside man for Gregory Rockwell. I know what I heard."

"I think you better get your hearing checked."

"You think so, Dawson?" I ticked my comments off on my fingers. "One, he mentioned Zacarelli by name. Two, he told him to stay in the barn, which has to be where they're hiding. Three, he mentioned not caring what they did with the girl. Four, and this is the big one, I actually heard him say the words 'kill the governor'. When I heard those words I confronted him but he attacked me. Kyle found me out cold on the ground. We ran back here and called Kohler's office. Theopolis intercepted the call and cut us off. I tried to call back and it just rang." My eyes drilled into Dawson. "If you don't believe me then check with the security guard. We all saw Theopolis get off the elevator by the security desk. As soon as he laid eyes on Kyle and me, he took off like a rocket. That was when I knew he was the guy. A guard chased him right out the door. By the time we got outside it was all over." The room was filled with murmurs. "So, if you tell me everything you just heard doesn't add up, then I'm going to tell you the governor doesn't have a chance in hell of staying alive with you people in charge!" An outraged Larry Dawson jumped to his feet.

"That's enough!" Kohler said. "Sit down, both of you." Dawson and I reluctantly took our seats, never taking our eyes off each other. "Let's assume for the moment that what Mr. Patterson has told us is true." Dawson began to interrupt but Kohler cut him off.

FBI agent Susan Kazakova spoke up. "Get me his phone and we'll take a look at the numbers Theopolis was communicating with. We'll also run a background check. Maybe something will pop up." She glanced toward Frank Genovese. "Frank can run a parallel investigation through Homeland Security."

"Lieutenant Dawson," Kohler said, "would you have one of your people get over to the hospital and retrieve Theopolis's cell phone?" Dawson grudgingly nodded and stepped away from the conference table. "Get the cell phone to Ms. Kazakova along with the rest of his personal belongings as soon as possible."

Yes, sir," Dawson said. If looks could truly kill, I would have been a dead man.

"Not sure Dawson's going to go out of his way to help us," Kyle whispered.

"He was never that helpful." I put my hand on Kyle's shoulder. "I always figured you and I were the guys who were going to get Megan back safe and sound. And I still believe that." As attendees began to file out of the meeting room, I rose from my seat, stretched, and let loose a well-deserved yawn. "Let's go."

Kyle stood, checking his watch. "It's one-thirty in the morning. Where are we off to now?"

"We'll crash at my place for a little while, maybe get some shut-eye if we can."

Chapter Thirty-Two
South of County Road 16, Nassau, NY
Ten miles southeast of Albany, NY
July 3, 2:03 AM

A white-hot stab of pain lanced through Megan's right arm. Her scream was swallowed by the night. Her breath came in short, ragged gasps.

Megan pushed herself slowly out from under a bush. Lying on her back, she gazed at the flickering stars spread across the night sky.

I was in a barn. When Megan touched her arm, her fingers came away feeling wet, sticky. *I was chained.* Her hand patted her blazer pocket, feeling the brooch. *This is how I got away.* The details refused to become clear without a fight. She hit someone, then ran away. Three loud bangs. Something struck her from behind and she fell down into a pit of darkness. She woke up here. But where was here? The sleeve of her blazer was torn. *I think I've been shot.*

Megan levered herself up to a sitting position. She sat for a few minutes, dizzy and light-headed. When the vertigo-like sensation slowed, she propelled her slim frame to her feet. The wobbling feeling started again.

Staggering to a nearby tree, she kept murmuring, "Stay still, it will pass."

Megan Fitzpatrick was on her feet and, more or less, ready to move. But which way? She had no idea from which direction she had come, nor which way to go. She saw no clues in the pitch darkness, but heard what could have been the sound of a passing vehicle, barely detectable in the distance. *If that was a car, then there's a road. And if there's a road, someone will find me. All I have to do is get there.*

* * *

Megan Fitzpatrick emerged from a patch of thick foliage onto a one-lane dirt road. She had no idea how long she had been walking. Her right arm throbbed, still bleeding. In the blackness, Megan saw nothing that would help her choose which way to go. She let fate decide. *Fate told me to turn left. I hope you know what you're doing.* Pushing off from a stout tree, she stumbled down the narrow dirt road. With an unsteady step, she slammed into something and fell to her knees.

It was an old dented mailbox covered in flaking green paint and splotched with rust, sitting at a drunken angle atop a post made from a thick tree branch. *What the hell?* Cracked flagstones led from the mailbox, the path disappearing into the black. Megan's exhausted mind did its best to unscramble what she had found. *An old mailbox in the woods? A flagstone path? To what?*

With new resolve, Megan laid her good arm across the mailbox and pulled herself to her feet. Her bloody handprint was a stark contrast to the rust and flaking paint. She took tentative steps, not wanting to fall in the darkness; it was becoming increasingly more difficult to get up every time she fell. Her unsteady feet dragged along the cracked and shifted flagstones.

Without warning, her foot hit a step. Her groping fingers touched a rough wooden handrail. Megan lifted her foot, mounting the first step, her hand sliding up the rail. She carefully took the next step, then the third, onto the small porch of a darkened cabin.

Megan pounded her fist against the door, reigniting the pain in her wounded arm. "Help! Please, help me!" No response. She kicked the door with her foot. "Is anyone there? Please. I've been shot." The doorknob was old and covered in scratches. There was no place to insert a key. Above it was a new deadbolt with a key cylinder. To get inside the cabin, she had to get through the deadbolt.

Megan slid down with her back against the door. There was a porch swing on the right, two old Adirondack chairs on the left, and a stack of split firewood next to the door. *If someone won't let me in, I'll let myself in.* She struggled to her feet, grabbed a piece of firewood, and slammed it against the window bordering the door. *Damn!* She swung a second time, as hard as a wounded, exhausted right-hander could swing left-handed. "Come on, you sonofabitch! Let me in!" Megan reared back, summoned her remaining strength, and smashed the firewood against the window.

The glass shattered, and the log dropped into the room with a loud clunk. Megan fell back onto the porch swing, trying to quell the pain tearing through her wounded arm.

Move. Megan's eyelids closed. *Move.* The rhythmic squeak of the swaying porch swing provided a lullaby. *Move, damn it!* She had to get inside and find help.

Megan rose and lurched toward the broken window. Reaching her good arm through the shattered pane, she groped for the deadbolt on the inside of the door. As her fingers explored, she managed to twist the thumbturn on the inside of the deadbolt. She was rewarded with the sound of the latch bolt clicking open. She turned the knob and pressed her good shoulder against the door. It swung open on protesting hinges, the rasping squeal scaring her.

"Hello?" No response came from the dark interior of the small cabin. "Is anyone here?" She took a tentative step over the threshold and ran her hand across the wall to the side of the doorway, searching for a light switch, finally finding one. Dim light from an old lamp sitting on an end table gave her enough light to take in her surroundings.

Mismatched, thrift shop furnishings filled the room. It was clear that this was nothing more than a weekend or vacation retreat. The knotty pine walls were covered with cheap travel posters and scruffy carpets lay upon the wood floors.

Megan stood in a small living room. A short, squat woodstove sat in one corner, with a well-worn couch and two overstuffed armchairs facing it. To the right was a tiny kitchen. Across from the front door was a short hallway.

"Hello? Is anyone here?" Megan moved toward the hallway. She found another light switch. A small glass globe on the hallway ceiling highlighted the shadows of dead insects trapped inside. There was a doorway on each side of the corridor and a third at the end.

Megan moved slowly, her sluggish gait a result of exhaustion more than caution. She glanced into a bedroom containing a queen-size bed and dresser. Megan peered into the room across the hallway. A smaller bedroom with bunk beds, a nightstand, and bookcase.

At the end of the corridor was a tiny bathroom. A

medicine cabinet with a mirrored front hung above a vanity. She caught a glimpse of herself in the mirrored door and froze, not recognizing the person staring back at her.

Her face was dirty after...how many days? Her raven black hair was frizzy and dull, her green eyes bloodshot. The suit she loved was grimy and wrinkled. Megan shook herself and focused on the wound.

The right shoulder of her blazer was torn, the entire sleeve soaked with blood. She let it fall to the floor. The white shirt was no better, also torn and bloodstained. She fumbled the buttons open with her left hand and let the shirt drop. Megan turned the water on, adjusting the faucets until it flowed warm, then grabbed a towel from the shelf and ran it under the faucet. Next, she took a roll of gauze, a box of adhesive bandages, and a bottle of aspirin from the medicine cabinet and placed them on the vanity top.

Megan prayed her wound looked worse than it really was. The bullet had just missed ripping through her shoulder, instead tearing open a large gash along the outside of her arm. She dabbed at the seeping blood with the warm, damp towel, repeatedly rinsing the blood off in the sink. It was a slow process; every time the towel touched her skin the pain was intense. The bowl of the sink was streaked with red as she continued to clean her wound and rinse the towel.

Satisfied, she dropped the blood-stained towel and fumbled with the box of adhesive bandages, dumping its contents on the vanity top. She peeled the backing off the 2" x 4" strips and stretched them across the ragged gash. The pain and blood made her dizzy; she hung her head to keep from passing out. She wrapped the entire length of gauze around her arm, tying off the end using her teeth and left hand. Blood seeped through the gauze.

Megan washed her hands, then popped the top off the aspirin bottle and shook a few tablets out onto the vanity top. She placed three tablets on her tongue, then used her left hand to scoop water into her mouth. Grabbing a washcloth off the shelf, she ran it under the faucet and scrubbed the grime off her face.

Megan found an old plaid shirt hanging on the back of the bathroom door. She lifted the shirt off the hook and shrugged into it, wincing from the movement of her wounded arm.

Shuffling down the hallway on leaden feet, she explored the bedrooms, finding nothing at all in the small closets. In the tiny kitchen, there was nothing in the refrigerator, nor was there anything in the cupboard. It didn't look like the cabin had been used so far this season. She made her way back to the living room where she noticed an old owl-shaped clock hanging on the knotty pine wall above the woodstove, its hands unmoving. She still had no idea what day or time it was. There was no television or computer in the cabin. To Megan's disappointment, there were no telephones either, which didn't surprise her since most people in this day and age were giving up landlines in favor of cell phones.

With a great sigh, Megan plopped down upon the lumpy couch. The front door was still wide open. She listened to the sounds of night creatures. The events of the last few days had drained her. She couldn't summon the strength to get herself off the couch to close the door. *To hell with it.*

Gazing around the dimly-lit room, she decided to wait until daylight, then venture out to find help. For now, she needed to rest. Megan had absolutely nothing left in her tank. Unraveling the mystery of Gregory and his henchmen would have to wait until daybreak.

She reached into her pocket, her fingers closing around a relic from her past that had saved her today. She slipped the brooch Rick Patterson had given her out of her pocket and stared at it. *I wonder what you're doing right now, Rick.*

She glanced at her gauze-wrapped upper arm. Satisfied she did all she could, Megan Fitzpatrick slumped to her side and fell into the deepest, most well-deserved slumber of her life, the brooch from Rick Patterson gripped tightly in her left hand.

Chapter Thirty-Three
Abandoned farm
Thirteen miles southeast of Albany, NY
July 3, 5:57 AM

Dawn broke, deep oranges and pinks painting the lightening sky. It was another beautiful summer morning in rural upstate New York, perfect in every way, except for the New York State Police Special Operations Response Team (SORT) slipping silently through the tangle of deep green foliage surrounding the barn where Megan Fitzpatrick had been held captive.

By the time the last team member moved into position, they had created an impenetrable barrier around the old structure, virtually invisible in their camouflage fatigues. An infrared scan of the building revealed no hot spots but the troopers were not going to take any chances.

Three troopers crept toward the chained wooden doors, two with automatic rifles at the ready, a third with bolt cutters to snip the lock. They eased the doors open a crack, tossed in a trio of M84 stun grenades, and darted behind the cover of the doors. The earsplitting bangs were accompanied by brilliant flashes of light. With their weapons at the ready, the troopers yanked the doors open. "Police! Drop your weapons!"

* * *

Kyle and I were back in the packed meeting room in the Capitol building after catching a few hours of fitful sleep on the couches in my office over *Tommy G's*. One of the techies told me that Homeland Security had used Theopolis's cell phone to pinpoint the barn where they believed Rockwell and Zacarelli had stashed Megan Fitzpatrick. Said they used what he referred to as "classified wizardry", the nuts and bolts of which they refused to divulge to the other agencies in the room. I guess the big kids still hadn't learned to play nice together. Unfortunately, the cell number assumed to be Gregory Rockwell's was from a burner phone. It appeared he had shut it down and removed the battery to keep it from being tracked. This guy had done his homework. Once the barn was located, the New York State Police assembled their SORT personnel and moved into position to storm the structure.

We watched the monitor as the scene at the abandoned barn unfolded. The array of smaller windows on the screen had been minimized allowing the video being transmitted from a trooper's helmet camera to fill the entire display. The sound of competing voices came from the speakers on either side of the screen.

I stared at the jostling image, hoping against all odds that I would see a healthy Megan Fitzpatrick being hustled out. We waited. The outline of a car emerged from the thinning wisps of smoke created by the stun grenades. I saw more troopers move into the barn from the edges of the screen. Multiple voices yelled, "Clear!" as their assault rifle-mounted flashlights swept the dark areas inside.

"Check for explosives!" the team leader, Lieutenant Lori Chun called out. Images emerged from her helmet cam. A moment later her voice reported there was no one in the barn. One day left and I still hadn't found Megan. Kyle buried his face in his hands. *He can't take much more of this*, I thought. *He isn't alone.*

Once the structure had been deemed safe, Chun called for a team to get inside and process the scene. They examined the interior of the structure, focusing on the workbench and abandoned car. I paced, another Styrofoam cup of cold, bitter coffee in my hand. All I could do was wait. And I was sick and tired of waiting. I had done it for days. Now I needed to get out in the field and find Megan.

A tall, burly trooper, Captain Jim Stallworth, was Chun's commander. He sat at the far end of the conference table in the Capitol building meeting room. Suddenly, Chun's voice came through one of those space-age-style speakerphones one of the techies had set up on the middle of the conference table. "Sir, no one is here. We did positively identify Anthony Zacarelli's fingerprints inside the vehicle. Also, we have found a large number of metal shavings and discarded snips of wiring consistent with materials used in the construction of pipe bombs. We're still checking for any traces of explosives."

"Anything to indicate a hostage was there?" said Stallworth.

"Possibly, sir." As Chun spun around, the inside of the barn came into view. A chill ran through me as her helmet cam swept across a long piece of chain with a manacle attached to it. The other end was secured to a sturdy looking support post. A pile of discarded food wrappers and water bottles lay nearby. "We have dried blood on this chain and manacle." Chun pointed but did not touch either item. "We'll get it tested ASAP." Right then and there I vowed to beat the shit out of Gregory Rockwell if I ever got close enough. "We're checking tire tracks and footprints inside and outside the barn. And I've dispatched a team to scour the grounds around our position."

"Good work," Stallworth said. "Keep me updated." The investigation continued to play out on the large screen. The room grew quiet. All eyes were on Stallworth. "I'm sure you all heard Chun's report. We may be looking at more explosive devices—"

"And looking for Megan Fitzpatrick, too," I said, not giving a damn about who I was interrupting. Too many long days and too little sleep had stretched my nerves as far as they were going to go. It seemed that Helen Clifton was the main priority to everyone in the room, maybe their only priority, and getting Megan back mattered only to Kyle and me.

"Of course, locating the female hostage—"

I cut Stallworth off. "She has a name."

Captain Stallworth looked like he was about to tear me apart. "Locating Megan Fitzpatrick is still as much a part of our operation as is apprehending the individuals responsible for placing the bombs on the *Slater*."

"I needed to hear she was still important to someone other than Kyle and me."

"Mr. Patterson, you—" Whatever Stallworth was going to say was cut short as Chun came back on the line.

"Sir, we found a trail of blood a short distance from the barn. It's being collected now. Also, three shell casings. We'll check them for prints."

"Okay, Chun," Stallworth said. "If this guy didn't police his brass, maybe he got sloppy on something else."

"Yes, sir." The line went dead.

Stallworth went back to staring at me. "We will continue to search for any sign of Ms. Fitzpatrick. I give you my word."

"That's all I ask."

* * *

We didn't have to wait long before Chun reported in. She told Captain Stallworth that they had managed to lift partial prints off the shell casings. This trooper knew her stuff. Homeland Security ran with the prints. Frank Genovese was notified of their owner within fifteen minutes. In spite of the prints not being complete, there was enough to give them a match. Technology was a wonderful thing when it worked.

Genovese stood next to the wall monitor as two pictures appeared side by side. The one on the left was from a military ID showing a young man, while the other was a mug shot of an older version of the same guy. "The prints from the three shell casings belong to Philip David Crowley, male, 31. Former military, dishonorably discharged, and like Anthony Zacarelli, a drifter with priors. And also like Zacarelli, we have no current whereabouts."

Counting the inside man who'd gotten creamed by the pizza delivery driver, this newest guy made four. I couldn't help but wonder just how big Gregory Rockwell's gang was.

Chapter Thirty-Four
South of County Road 16, Nassau, NY
Eleven miles southeast of Albany, NY
July 3, 7:38 AM

"What in the hell?" Gary Williams tapped the brake pedal of his Subaru wagon. The vehicle, towing a fishing boat, came to a stop in front of his small cabin. The recent retiree hadn't planned on opening his cabin for at least another two weeks; he was just dropping off his new fishing boat, a retirement gift to himself, ahead of time. Williams stared at the wide open front door. He could see a lamp burning farther back in the room. *Some sonofabitch broke into my cabin.*

Williams shouted through the open driver's side window, "If you're still in there, I'm gonna kick your ass!" No response. Then he noticed the shattered window next to the front door. Now he was really pissed off. Williams cupped his hands around his mouth and yelled again. "Hey! You in there! I'm comin' in and you're gonna be sorry!" Still no response.

Front door wide open, light on, broken window, and nobody coming out to see who the hell is yelling. "Well, isn't that the damnedest thing." Williams thought maybe the guilty party had taken off already. At least he hoped they had. He wasn't a young man anymore and would surely come out on the wrong end of a scuffle. He shut down the car's engine, opened the door, and hauled his bulky 62-year-old frame out of the small car. He hesitated, having second thoughts, then reached into the back seat and snatched up a crowbar. *Just in case.*

Williams crept along the old flagstone path, stopping at the foot of the porch steps. Grabbing the railing, he glanced around. Nothing. He climbed the three steps and stopped before the open door.

Williams glared at the broken window. "If you're still in there, you better come out now!" Williams cautiously stuck his head through the doorway.

"Last chance!" He took one step over the threshold and froze. Someone was laying on his old couch. "Hey!" He strode toward the couch, crowbar raised.

"What are you doing in my cab—" He stopped in mid-stride, shocked to see it was a young girl, barely 110 pounds, wearing his old work shirt. Her bandaged upper arm hung over the edge of the couch. The gauze was wet with blood, a few glistening spots had collected on the wood floor.

Megan Fitzpatrick stirred, but was unable to fight her way to full consciousness. "Help...me...please."

Williams dropped the crowbar and sank to his knees beside the couch. "What the hell happened to you?"

"Shot me," she mumbled. "Help..."

Williams didn't know what to do. His tired knees cracked as he struggled to his feet. "Stay right here. I'll get help." He moved toward the door, patting his pockets, searching for his cell phone. "Where the hell is that damn thing?" Failing to find his phone, he shouted, "I gotta go to my car and grab my phone! I'll be right back."

Williams hustled out to his car and checked all the usual places. His phone was nowhere to be found. He tried to recall if he even took it with him when he left his home that morning. Williams dropped into his car, started the engine, and backed his boat and trailer onto an empty patch of ground off the road. He got out and disconnected the trailer. There was a small clinic about five miles away in the tiny town of Nassau. Since he couldn't find his cell phone to call for help, he would drive this mystery girl there himself. He could contact the county sheriff once he got into town.

Williams rushed back to the cabin, nearly tripping as he ascended the steps. He shook the young woman gently. "Can you get up?" he whispered. "I'm gonna get you to Doc Westin's in town. She'll fix you up real good." When Megan didn't respond, he eased her into a sitting position. Her eyes remained closed and her head wobbled. "Can you tell me your name at least?" Her only reply came in the form of moans and grimaces.

"I'm sorry if I'm hurting you but I gotta get you out to my car." After much effort, Williams finally had her on her feet and moving toward the door. "C'mon, keep moving. You can do it," he said softly as they passed through the front door and onto the porch.

Williams hesitated at the top of the steps leading down to the flagstone path. "Three steps down, little girl, then we're in my car and on our way." Megan slumped against him, her feet barely supporting her. He tried to hold her up with one hand on the railing to steady himself. Just as Megan's feet hit the ground, her legs collapsed. She fell back on the steps, taking Williams down with her. He hit with a loud grunt.

"Okay," he whispered as they sat hunched together

on the bottom step. "We can rest here, but only for a minute." He kept his arm around her, rocking slowly back and forth. Finally, he pulled Megan to her feet. "Time to go, little girl."

Williams dragged Megan along the flagstone path. He just had to make it a couple more feet and they would be at the car. "C'mon, darlin', work with me here." His breathing was labored. The pounding of his heart made him wonder if he had remembered to take his blood pressure meds that morning.

Finally reaching his vehicle, Williams pinned Megan up against the side and yanked the rear door open. He backed her in, trying hard not to hurt her wounded arm. He got her on the seat, then ran around to the other side, and eased her in. He heaved himself into the driver's seat. A shudder ran through him; a wide smear of Megan's blood stretched across the front of his old T-shirt. Williams glanced at his cabin as the engine roared to life. The front door was still wide open. *Too late to worry about it now.*

"Hold tight, darlin'. I'm gonna get you help." Williams cranked the wheel and pulled onto the road leading from his remote cabin to County Road 16. The one-lane dirt road would make the going slow, but with luck he could be in Nassau in under ten minutes. From the back seat, Megan moaned with every pothole Williams failed to avoid.

* * *

Nine minutes later, Williams sped along Elm Street in the town of Nassau. He passed through the intersection with Church Street as the light turned yellow, eliciting an angry honk from a car he cut off, then skidded to a halt in front of a large home that had been converted to a doctor's office. Williams pounded the horn half a dozen times, then tumbled out of his car just as a young man in blue scrubs stuck his head out the front door.

"Help me!" Williams shouted. "I got an injured girl here!"

The male nurse bolted out the door. "Doctor," he called back to the house. "We need help out here!" He eased Williams aside so he could get to the injured woman. "What happened to her?" he asked.

"Damned if I know," Williams said. "I went to my cabin this morning and found the front door wide open and one of my windows busted. There she was, lying on my couch."

"Was she able to tell you anything?"

"Nothing. Don't know her name or who she is. She mighta said she got shot."

"Is this your handiwork?" He motioned toward the bloody gauze wrapped around Megan's arm.

"Nope. That's how I found her."

Dr. Westin rushed out of the house. "What have we got?"

"Possible gunshot wound to the upper arm," said the nurse.

"Exam room number two," said Dr. Westin. The nurse carried Megan inside. Williams stood by his car unsure of what he was supposed to do now. Dr. Westin waved him in and motioned to a chair in the small waiting room. "Please wait here."

"Sure, Doc." Williams dropped heavily onto a thinly cushioned chair and nudged his soiled bucket hat off his brow. He took a tissue from a nearby table and wiped the perspiration from his forehead. There was a small flat-screen television mounted on the wall of the waiting room, tuned to the local all-news station. The sound was too low for Williams to hear, but the image on the screen caught his attention.

Three pictures stretched across the screen: two men and one woman. He rose and moved closer. Williams squinted at the three faces staring back at him. He pulled his glasses out of his T-shirt pocket and slipped them on, then zeroed in on the young woman, examining her closely. "Well, ain't this been a helluva day," he said. "Doc! I think you better see this right away!" Unless his old eyes were lying to him, it was the same girl he had just brought into Doc Westin's office.

Chapter Thirty-Five
Albany, NY
July 3, 10:21 AM

Lieutenant Chun was no longer in the barn. In fact, the scene had changed completely. The barn was gone. A small cabin filled the screen. "Sir, we were able to follow someone's tracks from the barn to this cabin. Distance looks to be almost two miles north of the barn. Tracks could be a young woman's. The front door was open when we arrived and one of the windows has recently been broken. No one was around. We're processing the scene now, sir."

The helmet cam zeroed in on the open door and busted window. The image moved up the steps, across the porch, and through the front doorway. Dark stains splattered the floor and shabby couch. The image moved to the end of the hallway and stopped just inside the bathroom, taking in the sink and floor. "Someone tried to fix themselves up here." Chun's gloved hand moved into the frame. She pointed at the torn, bloody blazer and blouse in a pile on the floor. "We have a woman's blazer and blouse covered in blood."

"Those are Megan's!" Kyle shot to his feet. He stared at his sister's clothes, then sagged back down. "Oh, God, no..."

I rested my hand on the back of his neck. "Kyle, she's not there which means she's probably still okay." I wasn't ready to give up on her yet.

Kyle stared at me through tired, bloodshot eyes. "But the blood—how in the hell can you be so sure, Rick? They've had her for days and this is all we've found of her."

"You have to trust me, Kyle."

Captain Stallworth told Chun to contact him with any new information. He stepped around the table and stood over Kyle. My friend sobbed softly. I didn't know what else I could say to reassure him. I looked up at Stallworth. The big trooper nodded at me, then placed his hand on Kyle's shoulder.

"I believe there is still hope," Stallworth said. Kyle's moist eyes pleaded with Stallworth to mean what he was saying. "Let's wait for Chun to finish her job and we'll go on from there, okay?" Kyle nodded half-heartedly. He was wiped out, pretty much ready to crash and burn.

APD Lieutenant Larry Dawson's cell phone beeped.

"Dawson, here." His eyes grew wide. "When did the call come in?" The room went silent. "And they're sure? Absolutely positive?" he asked. "Dispatch a couple of cars and an ambulance right now." He listened again, then shouted into the phone. "I said right now!" Thirty agonizing seconds passed. "Okay," said Dawson. "And let Albany Med know they have a patient inbound." He dropped his phone on the polished surface of the conference table, then addressed Kyle.

"We've located your sister."

Kyle blanched. I wondered if Dawson was about to

break bad news. "She's alive and in good condition," he said.

I jumped in. "Where is she?"

"The cabin that was broken into?" Dawson said, momentarily forgetting our differences. "Sure enough it was her. The owner happened to come by and found her passed out inside. He didn't have a phone so he loaded her into his vehicle and rushed her to Nassau. He got her to a doctor's office there, a Doctor Michelle Westin, and she patched up Megan."

"And *patched up* means?" I asked. Kyle looked afraid to hear the answer.

"Westin says Megan was shot—"

"Jesus!" Kyle lurched to his feet. He swayed drunkenly. "Shot? Somebody shot my sister?" His hands shook. "I'm gonna kill those bastards! I swear—"

"That's enough, man!" I grabbed him by the arms. As far as I was concerned, I had let him blow off enough steam. "They said Megan's going to be okay. What she needs now is to see you at Albany Med when she arrives. She doesn't need to worry about you locking horns with these maniacs. You leave that to us."

I turned to Stallworth. "Can you get him over to the hospital?"

Dawson spoke up. "I have a couple of guys I can spare."

I nodded. Although I was still wary of him, I decided to return the favor and play nice. "Thanks, Lieutenant. Any chance they can stay there with him?"

"Yeah, sure." Dawson got to his feet. "I'll even take him down personally."

When our eyes met, I released my grip on Kyle. It seemed his storm had passed. "Kyle, go with Lieutenant Dawson. He'll make sure you get to Albany Med," I said.

"Take care of Megan."

"Why don't you come with me?" Kyle asked. "Megan deserves to know what you did for her."

"Rick still has work to do here." Andy Kohler had been quietly observing from the corner of the room. "As soon as we have this situation wrapped up, I'll get him there. I promise."

I wasn't sure what Kohler had in mind but curiosity kept me from saying anything that might muddy up the waters. "Go ahead, Kyle," I said. "I'll get there as soon as I can." The expression on Dawson's face told me he was also trying to figure out what Kohler meant by wanting me to stick around. Was I about to piss someone off again?

Kohler waved at me to follow him as the rest of the room got back to business; voices grew louder and fingers attacked keyboards. There were still three loose cannons somewhere in the area. Until they were contained, the governor's life was in danger. I stepped into the hallway where Kohler was waiting.

"Let's walk, Rick." Something told me I was going to have the boom lowered on me. Again. "I understand you had applied to work in the auxiliary protection detail on the day of the governor's announcement?"

"That was my plan," I said. "But I got bounced out at the last minute."

"By?"

"Dawson."

"Any particular reason?"

"I worked under him when I was a police officer here in Albany." I really didn't want to revisit that part of my life so I left it at that.

"And?"

Damn. There was no getting around this. "And my partner

was shot and killed one night on patrol. He was a real popular guy, a cop's cop. Anyway, I was cleared of any wrongdoing but Dawson has had it out for me ever since." I shrugged my shoulders. "That's pretty much it."

Andy Kohler crossed his arms. "Tell you what. I'd like to hire you as auxiliary protection for the governor while she's aboard the *Slater.*" His offer knocked me off my feet. "Well?" he said.

"I'd like that," I said. "But what about Lieutenant Dawson? I know he's going to have an issue with my being there."

"It's not up to Dawson how I take care of Governor Clifton. I ran a full background check on you and there's no reason you shouldn't be on the security detail. Hell, if it wasn't for you being such a pain in my ass, I don't think we'd have gotten as far as we have identifying the bombers." He extended his hand. "So, you in?"

I gripped his hand. "You bet I am."

"Excellent!" Kohler said. "I suggest you get over to Albany Med and check on your friends. Get back here by 7:00 PM. Security assignments will be handed out for the governor's rally tomorrow."

"See you at seven," I said. "And thanks, Andy. You have no idea how much this means to me."

As I left the building I couldn't help but believe that this was one of those rare occasions in life when you got a second chance. My mind was made up; on this detail, there was no way in hell that I would fail.

Chapter Thirty-Six
Albany Medical Center
Albany, NY
July 3, 1:51 PM

"I'm gonna grab something at the cafeteria." APD Officer Dave Witkowski got to his feet. "You want anything?"

"Nah," his partner, Steve Flynn, said. "I'll stay here and babysit him." He jerked a thumb in the direction of Kyle Fitzpatrick, sitting sullenly in the waiting room. "This guy's a real downer."

Flynn was bored out of his mind. He had no problem transporting Kyle Fitzpatrick to Albany Medical Center, but having to sit there was killing him. With three potential bombers roaming the city, he wanted to be out there enjoying the thrill of the hunt. His lieutenant, Larry Dawson, had decided otherwise.

"Suit yourself, partner," Witkowski said. "I'll be back in a few." He turned to Kyle. "Hey, you want something to eat or drink?" Kyle shook his head and went back to staring at the floor tiles between his feet. Witkowski glanced at Flynn and shrugged. "Whatever," he said, then strode down the long hallway in search of the cafeteria.

"Yeah, whatever," Flynn said. It was time to move on to something more entertaining than watching this guy mope. Flynn had his eye on an attractive, young RN manning the nurses station just down the corridor. "Well, hello, you pretty little thing," he cooed softly to himself. He smoothed down the front of his uniform shirt and straightened his tie. *Looks like this could be your lucky day, Steve.* He glanced at Kyle. Deciding his charge was fine sitting alone for a while, Flynn strode to the nurses station, easing right up to the counter next to the nurse he had set his sights on.

Flynn turned on his trademark 10,000-watt, gleaming smile. "So, what's a poor, sick boy have to do to get some loving care around here?"

* * *

I caught up to Kyle at Albany Med around 2:15 PM. After wandering aimlessly from one nurses station to another, I finally found him sitting in a small waiting area by himself. He was slouched in an uncomfortable chair, hands clasped in his lap, staring at the floor between his outstretched feet. Dave Witkowski sat in the corner of the room, cap pulled down over his eyes, arms folded across his chest. The guy was supposed to be watching out for Kyle but instead was catching forty winks. Farther down the corridor his partner, Steve Flynn, was trying to charm a young RN out of her scrubs. This guy never quit. He was graced with the looks of a model while cursed with the personality of a road apple.

I dropped into the chair next to Kyle. "Hey, buddy."

"Rick! I'm so glad to see you, man."

"What's up with Megan? Have you seen her yet?"

"Only when they wheeled her in. She was unconscious." He lowered his voice. "She doesn't know

I'm here."

"Anybody talk to you about her condition?"

"The doctor said she was stable. Said he'd be back when he knew more." Kyle yawned. "Jesus, Rick, I don't think I've ever been so exhausted."

"Megan's safe now. It's okay for you to rest. Stretch out on a sofa and catch a few winks. I can hang here with you for a while."

Just then, an attractive middle-aged woman wearing a white coat approached. She fiddled with the stethoscope draped around her neck. "Mr. Fitzpatrick?" she asked.

Kyle got to his feet. "Yes, I'm Kyle Fitzpatrick."

"Ah, good." She swept her hand toward his chair. "Please, sit, Mr. Fitzpatrick." She now looked at me. "If you would excuse us, I'd like to speak to Mr. Fitzpatrick about his sister."

I stood to leave. Kyle grabbed my arm and pulled me back down. "This is Rick Patterson. He's with me," he said. "And please call me Kyle."

"Alright then, Kyle."

"How's my sister?"

"Megan's going to be fine," she said softly. "Have they told you what happened?"

"Not really."

"I'll try to fill in all the blanks." She smiled. "First, I'm Doctor Michelle Westin. I have a medical practice in Nassau. Megan was discovered injured in a cabin not too far from me. Lucky for your sister, the gentleman who owned the cabin happened to stop by, found her, and rushed her to my office. While I was treating her, we realized she was the girl on the news who was missing. We contacted the police right away and here we are."

"And she'll be fine?" I asked.

"Her injuries are not life-threatening, however, she

did go through quite a bit of trauma and lost a fair amount of blood. She's heavily sedated and resting comfortably now. She should recover nicely."

"Was she shot, Doctor?" I asked.

"Yes, but it was not a serious wound." She turned to Kyle. "More of a close call. Probably no permanent damage beyond a scar."

"Thank God."

Dave Witkowski had woken up and from his corner seat was stretching the kinks out of his back. Steve Flynn, was still trying to convince the hot RN that he was a gift from Heaven sent to charm her. It didn't look good as she abruptly hustled away. He called after her, but she disappeared around a corner and was gone. Flynn hooked his thumbs in his belt and sauntered back toward Kyle and me. "Well, well. Look who wandered in. Here to see how the big boys do it?"

I remained in my chair. I was just too worn out to dance with this asshole.

"Knock it off, Steve," Witkowski called from the waiting area. "Dawson told you to play nice."

Flynn scowled, then stormed off. I figured he was on the hunt again. Jerks can't help but be what they are. Steve Flynn was living proof of that.

"Excuse me, Mr. Fitzpatrick?" A nurse in pink scrubs strode toward us.

"I'm Kyle Fitzpatrick." He straightened up in his chair.

"Your sister is settled in. You can see her, but be aware that she is still unconscious. She needs rest right now."

Kyle jumped to his feet. "Yes, thanks. I need to be sure she's okay."

"And this is?"

"Rick is on the team that helped find Megan. And he's my best friend."

Kyle and I trailed a few feet behind the nurse. A lot of medical people zipped up and down the corridors. I wondered if this was a busy day or normal. We crossed a number of intersecting hallways. Kyle and I hesitated before passing through afraid of colliding with the ever-present someone or something. The nurse leading us just shot right through every time.

We arrived at Megan's room. The nurse opened the door and stepped in, then held it open for us. "Remember to stay quiet," she said. "I'll be back in about ten minutes."

I stood just inside the door as Kyle hung at the foot of Megan's bed. I'm sure he was distressed by the sight of his baby sister unconscious in a hospital bed. She was hooked up to monitors that beeped and flashed. IVs snaked into her arms.

I slid beside Kyle and lay a reassuring hand on his shoulder. He trembled. I whispered, "It's okay, Kyle. She's safe now. All these things attached to her are just to monitor her condition."

Kyle didn't speak. A tear crept down his cheek. I moved a chair to the side of Megan's bed, then guided him to it. I backed up against the wall opposite the foot of Megan's bed, crossed my arms, and waited. I wanted so badly to touch Megan at that moment, to let her know I was there, that I still cared. I never liked hospitals. Always did whatever I could to avoid them. This time was different. I would have been happy to stay in that room with Megan until hell froze over.

A few minutes later the nurse stuck her head in. She raised her eyes in a way that said, *Is everything okay?* I nodded. She slid out of the room, the door closing behind her without a sound.

Kyle held Megan's hand, his head resting on their clasped hands. The room was silent except for the monitors playing their strange melody of beeps and tones. I focused on Megan from my spot against the wall. The white sheet covering her rose and fell slowly, rhythmically. Megan hadn't changed a bit since I'd last seen her. She was more beautiful than I remembered. Her raven black bangs hung loosely over her forehead. Even though her eyes were closed, I remembered them being the most brilliant shade of green I'd ever seen. And those same eyes had looked right into my very soul. I felt a flutter in my chest. Was there still something between us? Could I rekindle what I had once thought was the love of my life? How could I even think about that when she was lying in a hospital bed after going through such an ordeal?

I leaned against the wall, my arms folded across my chest. Kyle hadn't moved, still held his sister's hand, his head resting on their intertwined fingers. The door slowly opened. The nurse quietly stepped over to me. We both watched Kyle for a moment. She leaned in and whispered, "It's time."

I nodded and arched my back, pushing myself off the wall.

"You should probably get him to rest a little. He looks like he's ready to drop."

"I will," I said. "It's been a tough couple of days for him too."

She went to Kyle's side and gently nudged him. He lifted his head. "Time for you to go," she whispered. "Your friend is going to see that you get some rest."

Kyle kissed Megan's hand.

"One other thing, Mr. Fitzpatrick." The nurse reached into the nightstand and withdrew something. "I thought you might want to hold on to this." Her fingers opened outward like the petals of a flower. My knees weakened. I pressed my palm against the wall, steadying myself.

Kyle took the object from the nurse's hand and inspected it. "I don't—"

"It was the only personal item your sister had with her when she arrived. Even though she was unconscious, she was clutching it so hard we were barely able to open her fingers."

Kyle held it out to me. "What do you think?"

I felt like I had seen a ghost. My shaking hand took the brooch from Kyle and held it up to the light. It was nothing more than a delicate ring of bright silver about an inch and three-quarters in diameter. The inside contained a silver palm tree with green leaves made of shiny stones. There was a colorful toucan decorated with stones of blue, red, and yellow.

Staring at the object, I smiled. My eyes misted over. I struggled to control my emotions. It was the brooch I had surprised Megan with during a cruise in the Cayman Islands. I tried to think of a reason why it was the only personal item she had been found with. Seeing her again had weakened the walls I had built up around me after Megan had stormed out of my life years ago. Maybc that's why I believed this was a sign from some divine deity, that I was being given one more chance to make things right.

"There's a story behind this brooch, Kyle." My voice cracked as I tried to get the words out. I placed the brooch carefully in his hand, folding his fingers over it. "I'll tell you about it later. For now, keep it safe for Megan."

Kyle handed the brooch back to me. "Would you

take care of it? I can barely think straight right now."

I slipped it into my pocket.

"Time to go, guys," the nurse said. Kyle couldn't take his eyes from Megan. It seemed like he was afraid to leave. "She's fine, now," the nurse assured him. "Nothing to worry about. Go and take care of yourself." She glanced at me. I silently mouthed, *thank you*, and took Kyle by the elbow, guiding him out of the room. Back at the waiting area, we dropped back into the uncomfortable chairs. Kyle slumped and turned his face to the ceiling, eyes closed.

"All thing considered, Megan is doing well," I said. "She'll be up and out of here before you know it."

Kyle rocked his head slightly.

Time to change the subject. "Hey, you won't believe what happened right before I left Kohler a little while ago." Kyle glanced at me vaguely through red-rimmed eyes. His inability to focus told me he was about to go down for the count. I reconsidered for a moment, then said, "Maybe we'll talk after you get some rest."

"Go ahead. I'm just going to get comfortable here." Kyle leaned back and rested his feet on the opposite chair. "How can I thank you, Rick? You were the only guy who believed me. And you got Megan back, safe and sound, just like you said you would."

"Thanks, but it wasn't just me, ya know? There were a lot of people involved in getting Megan back."

"Nobody put their heart and soul into it like you did. And I'm going to make sure Megan knows." My hand rested on the brooch in my pocket. My heart fluttered again. Just seeing Megan made me believe I could rekindle our relationship.

Kyle yawned and sank a little lower in his chair. "You said something about big news?"

I laced my fingers together behind my head and gazed up at the ceiling. "Kohler asked me to be on the security detail tomorrow. Can you believe that?" Kyle responded with a deep snore. I looked over at him, amazed that someone could drop off so quickly. He had finally crashed. Good for him. I stepped over to the nurses station and got a blanket from a male nurse built like a linebacker. I covered Kyle. It was the first time he had been at peace since he called me just a couple of days ago.

"Sleep well, my friend," I said. "You've earned it." Neither of the APD officers assigned to keep an eye on him were around, so I dropped into the chair next to him. I decided there was time for me to watch over Kyle for a while as he slept.

My security meeting with Kohler wasn't until 7:00 PM. That gave me plenty of time to get back to my office for a shower and change of clothes. I made a mental note to check my pistol just in case. I had no reason to believe I'd need it tomorrow, but better safe than sorry.

Chapter Thirty-Seven
Albany, NY
July 3, 5:13 PM

The blue Ford Taurus came to a halt at the stop sign on the corner of Green and Rensselaer Streets in Albany's South End. Phil Crowley crouched behind the wheel, glancing around the intersection from behind dark sunglasses and a blue ball cap. NYPD in silver stitching adorned the front of his hat.

"I think this is a really bad idea," Tony Zacarelli said. He sported mirrored sunglasses along with a plain black ball cap and slouched so low in the front seat that Crowley wondered how he could even see over the dashboard. Zacarelli hadn't stopped fidgeting or whining since they left Crowley's hideout. The beating the girl in the barn gave him had taken the wind out of his sails.

"Shut the hell up and keep looking for barriers or road closed signs," Crowley snarled. "Mark them on the map. I need to know what streets are going to be blocked off tomorrow." He took one last look around the intersection before creeping through it. "I don't need to get trapped in a dead end." Crowley knew scouting the area around the USS *Slater* in broad daylight was a ballsy move, especially with the media broadcasting his face along with Rockwell's and Zacarelli's, but he believed the future rewards would far outweigh the risks.

Before he was dishonorably discharged from the army, Phil Crowley worked with small drones and had become adept at modifying and operating them. The recent glut of news stories on the increasing use of civilian drones is what had actually given birth to his twisted idea.

Every day there were stories of homeowners shooting at intrusive drones they believed were spying on their homes and families. The instances of drones playing chicken with low flying aircraft were also becoming daily items in the news. Law enforcement and military pundits repeatedly warned that drones could become the weapon of choice in the near future. They were easily attained, easy to operate, and totally unregulated. There was little or no defense against them and they were showing up more and more.

Crowley was using his attack on the USS *Slater* to test out the first of what he envisioned to be dozens of drone strikes. Once he successfully pulled off the attack on Governor Clifton, he planned to hire himself out to the highest bidders for future operations where his prowess with drones was required.

Rockwell and Zacarelli had no idea what Crowley was intending to do. And he had no intention of telling them. By the time tomorrow's festivities were over, his business, tentatively titled in his mind as *Deadly Drones For Hire*, would be a well-known, one-man, money-making operation.

Crowley slowed as he approached the next intersection. An APD officer stood on the corner next to a signpost. A large yellow placard with DETOUR in bold black letters above a black arrow pointing to the left was attached to the post right below the sign. As the vehicle came to a stop, the officer seemed to be staring at him. Without warning, the officer waved, then walked up to Crowley's side of the car. Crowley's hands gripped the wheel.

"Jesus!" Zacarelli hissed. "What's going on?" He slouched lower in the seat.

"Shut up!" Crowley said in a hushed voice. "Don't say a goddamn word." He unhooked the car's sun visor and swung it around so it blocked the top of the driver's side window. "Pull your hat down like your sleeping." Crowley lowered his window.

The APD officer was young and thin. He looked like he could have just graduated from high school. "Evening, Officer," Crowley said as he peeked below the visor. "How goes preparations for tomorrow?" He hoped the angle was enough to hide his face.

"No problems," the cop replied. He stepped back and glanced down at the front tire. "Were you aware your front tire is almost flat?"

Crowley couldn't believe his luck. This section of town was crawling with law enforcement personnel, and he had somehow been noticed by a rookie because of a flat tire. This kid had no idea who they were. "I didn't realize that, Officer. I'll get that taken care of right now."

The policeman looked through the windshield. "What's with him?"

"Thanks for pointing out our tire, Officer," Crowley said, pretending not to have heard the question. "I'm going right up to the tire store on Central Avenue to get it checked out."

"What's with your buddy?"

"He did a little too much celebrating last night." Crowley pointed to his T-shirt. He and Zacarelli both sported red T-shirts with *Team Clifton* logos on them. "Tomorrow's going to be a huge day for this country and we're a part of it."

The cop stepped back from the car. "Make sure you get that tire checked before it goes flat and you block the street. We're going to have enough traffic to worry about come tomorrow."

"Sure thing, Officer." Crowley pressed on the gas pedal, easing through the intersection.

"And keep an eye on your buddy. There are going to be a lot of DWI checkpoints set up."

Crowley gave the cop a thumbs up.

Zacarelli straightened up in his seat and nudged his hat further back on his head. "Sonofabitch!" He used the front hem of his *Team Clifton* T-shirt to mop the sweat from his brow.

"You gotta admit, grabbing a pair of these crappy T-shirts was a stroke of genius," Crowley said.

"Maybe," Zacarelli said. "I doubt we'll get that lucky again."

"No luck involved. Just my pair of big brass balls." Crowley grabbed his crotch and laughed. "We'll stop and fill the tire. It should be enough to get us through the next couple of hours until we dump this piece of crap and grab the van."

"I think our map is all set," Zacarelli said. "We can check the news for any last minute changes."

"Now you're talking like a believer," Crowley said. "All you gotta do tomorrow is follow the route I mark out for you. I'll handle the drone."

Zacarelli gazed out his window as Crowley drove the route that would eventually lead them out of Albany's

South End. Ragged children played on the sidewalks in front of dilapidated homes lining the street. He wondered if any of them would be near the USS *Slater* tomorrow when the bomb went off.

Zacarelli shook his head and breathed deeply. The sooner he got out of this city and away from this nut job behind the wheel, the better off he'd be. All he had to do was live through tomorrow.

Chapter Thirty-Eight
Albany, NY
July 3, 8:17 PM

"Information Technology staff will be here, here, and here," Albany Police Department Lieutenant Larry Dawson announced. He tapped three spots on the eighty-inch wall display. As if by magic, orange blocks sprouted on the screen where his finger had touched.

An overhead shot of the section of Albany where the USS *Slater* was docked filled the huge screen. The old warship rested in the center. Orange, yellow, blue, red, gray, and green blocks represented the assigned position of law enforcement and other agency members. Each color indicated the agency and each block contained a person's name and ID. The colored blocks were splashed not only on the USS *Slater*, but also throughout the neighborhood surrounding it. A grid overlaying the entire map with letters running along the top and numbers down the left side made me think of the old game *Battleship*.

The space-age depiction, resembling something right out of a *Star Trek* movie, was part of a cutting-edge system known as COPPS (Computer Oriented Personnel Positioning System). The Albany Police Department had been experimenting with COPPS and preliminary results had been excellent. This would be the first large-scale deployment of the system.

Dawson continued. "If anyone has a problem with their communications devices, the closest IT person will be dispatched immediately. Their goal will be to get you connected and back on the grid within two minutes."

Dawson examined a stack of sheets he held in his hand. He looked up and addressed the personnel jammed into the meeting room in the Capitol building. "Individual assignments will be handed out to your teams in the next meeting. All personnel will be outfitted with small tablets showing the same image you see on the wall display with everyone's position in real time. In addition, everyone will carry trackers that will constantly feed their current location into the computer system. As soon as the IT staff activates the tablets and trackers, individual names will appear in the various blocks. Also, everyone will be carrying standard radio equipment. Any questions?" Dawson waited a moment. "Good. You may all proceed down the hall to the rooms your teams have been assigned to. IT staff will be there to hand out equipment."

Personnel rose and filed out of the meeting room. Individuals peeled off from the stream of people flowing down the hall as they passed their assigned meeting rooms, each indicated by a doorway marked with an orange, yellow, blue, red, gray, or green placard.

* * *

Andy Kohler had attached me to the Albany Police Department. Following the line of law enforcement personnel moving down the hall, I saw a doorway with a large blue placard taped to the wall next to it. I swung into the room, found a seat along the far wall, and quietly settled in. Knowing how lucky I was to be a part of this operation, albeit last minute, I decided to sit where I wouldn't be noticed. A long string of strange events had gotten me here since my initial turn-down for this gig. All I wanted was to get my equipment and instructions, and show these guys I could do the job. I hoped a favorable outcome might lead to more of these security contractor assignments with the APD. I wasn't thinking too far beyond tomorrow's operation. Or the paycheck it would mean. If I didn't screw up, this could be the job that finally got my private investigation career moving in the right direction. And that would make a whole lot of my bill collectors happy.

From the far corner of the room, my eyes swept the crowd filtering in. I recognized some of the men and women from my short stint on the APD. Most looked me in the eye and nodded. I took those silent gestures to be greetings. I was okay with the lack of backslapping and fanfare for an old comrade-in-arms coming back temporarily into the fold. By nature I was a low profile kind of guy anyway.

Down the hall, Susan Kazakova was heading up the FBI team in the green-tagged room while Frank Genovese was lead man for the Department of Homeland Security group in the meeting room identified by the yellow placard. Albany Fire Department staff was farther down the hallway in the red-tagged room, while the last meeting room, marked by a gray-colored placard, was filled with New York State Troopers.

Everyone took a seat as Lieutenant Dawson entered the room. Two members of the IT staff, one male, the other female, followed Dawson in, maneuvering a small cart loaded with boxes. Moving to the side, they waited in silence. The IT people looked to be run-of-the-mill computer whiz kids; average height and build, and a bit on the pale side. They may not have looked like Greek gods, but these techies were the ones running our technology-riddled world. I guess given enough time, the meek really could inherit the earth.

Lieutenant Dawson spent the next hour going over individual assignments, procedures, and what to expect. After Dawson answered questions, he motioned for the IT gal to hand out tablets and trackers, while the IT guy entered the recipients' names into a database on his own tablet. I sat patiently and waited my turn. I would be stationed on the dock near the bow of the ship. Not the most glorious location, but I was happy to be there at all.

My cell phone vibrated softly against my chest. I slipped it out of my sport coat's inner pocket and checked the screen. A new text message from Kyle Fitzpatrick.

> *Megan stable & doing fine. Still in & out but knows I am here & what u did. MDs expect quick recovery. She would like to see u first chance u get. Good luck tomorrow. - KF*

I stared at the text message. Was the door to Megan opening a crack or was it my imagination wishing for another shot at the one that got away? I could not think of a valid reason why I never tried to get Megan back after she walked out on me. Sure, there were reasons, but not any that made me look good.

"Sir?"

I made a snap decision to get my butt over to Albany Medical Center to see Megan just as soon as I was released from tomorrow's events. If she was reaching out,

I would take her hand and breach that damn wall I had built around me after Dave Taylor had been killed on my watch.

"Excuse me, sir?"

The IT gal stood before me. I wondered how long she had been there. "Sorry." I jumped to my feet.

"No problem," she said. "I have your tablet and tracker here. I need your name and then we can activate it and link you into the system."

"Name's Rick Patterson." I held up my ID. "I'm one of the security contractors working with the APD."

She checked her list, found my name, then pulled a small tablet and a tracker from a box on her cart. Tapping away at the screen, she turned to the IT guy, gave him my name and rattled off a bunch of numbers that I assumed were some sort of identifiers for the tablet and tracker assigned to me.

"Here you go, Mr. Patterson." The IT gal hit something on the tablet and the screen came to life. I found myself looking down at the Capitol and the neighborhood around it. "I'm going to zoom out so you can see what happens when I turn on your tracker." She flicked the switch on my tracker and a small blue box appeared on the Capitol building. She zoomed in so I could see my name in the square. There were different colored boxes scattered all over the Capitol building as other trackers came to life. She turned my tracker off to alleviate the traffic jam of colored boxes on the screen. "Obviously, everyone will be spread out tomorrow so the boxes and IDs will be easier to see."

"Obviously," I said, trying to sound like I knew what she was talking about.

"Any questions?"

"Nope," I said. "Seems easy enough to me. Kind of

like an electronic leash for a dog."

She looked at me as if I was speaking a foreign language, then smiled. "Yes, I think that's a fair comparison."

IT gal placed my tablet and tracker in a small black zipper case. IT guy stuck a piece of gray duct tape on the case, and used a black marker to write my name on it. The zipper case went back into a large box containing similar cases on their cart. "Equipment will be distributed tomorrow morning from six numbered police vans parked along Washington Avenue," IT gal said. "You will pick up your equipment at 10:00 A.M. from van number two. At that time you will activate it and verify everything is working correctly. You will then be shuttled down to the site." She looked up at me. "Are there any questions, Mr. Patterson?"

"Sounds pretty clear to me," I said.

"Very good. See you at 10 A.M." I thanked IT gal and IT guy. They moved on to the next person, a female police officer chugging hot black coffee from a paper cup.

I stepped out of the room and strode down the hallway. I checked my watch. It was almost 9:30 P.M. Stopping at Albany Medical Center to see Megan was out of the question; visiting hours were over. And I guess I didn't want to seem too eager anyway. I thought about that and had to tell myself not to be an idiot. Again.

A rumble from my stomach told me I should stop at *Tommy G's* for dinner. From there I would head upstairs to my office/apartment and try to get some sleep. I figured tomorrow would be an exciting day and an opportunity to get my life and career back on track.

Chapter Thirty-Nine
Troy, NY
July 3, 10:05 PM

The Troy-Menands bridge had spanned the Hudson River since 1933. The old through-truss style bridge connected the Village of Menands in Albany County to South Troy in Rensselaer County. Just off the east end of the bridge sat South End Tavern, for decades a well-known eatery in South Troy. Opened in 1934, the restaurant was now an out-of-business, deteriorating hulk.

The blue Taurus came off the bridge, turned left off the main road, and pulled in alongside the old restaurant. Phil Crowley, sitting behind the wheel, toggled the vehicle's high beams on, then turned left, navigating the Taurus between a large blue Dumpster and a small green trash bin behind the building, the two banged-up receptacles long forgotten by the waste company printed on their sides. The white van they planned to use the next day for the attack on the USS *Slater* sat nearby, barely visible under a thick stand of low trees.

Crowley turned off the headlights and killed the engine. "Here we are." He swung his door open and eased out of the vehicle.

Gregory Rockwell got out of the back seat and looked around. "How the hell did you find this place?"

Tony Zacarelli slipped out of the front passenger seat and stared at the tall, dark building. "Is it even safe to go inside?"

"Trust me," Crowley said. "It ain't pretty, but it's the safest place for us to be right now. Nobody is going to look for us in there."

"You sound pretty confident," Rockwell said. He retrieved a large package wrapped in plain brown paper from the back seat. "Why's that?"

Crowley chuckled, then waved for the two men to follow him into the darkened structure. The center of the restaurant was three stories tall, sandwiched between a pair of two-story buildings. After making sure the rear door was secured, Crowley flicked a small flashlight on and led them to the third floor. All of the windows had been covered with heavy blankets to keep any light from leaking out and announcing their presence.

Crowley turned off his flashlight as he approached one of the rear windows. Lifting the corner of the blanket covering the dirty, cracked glass, he pointed to a nearby building. It was large, stark, and brightly lit. A tall chain link fence topped with razor wire surrounded the rear section. "See those lights over there? That's the Rensselaer County Sheriff's Office and Correctional Facility." He laughed again. "We're hiding from the cops right in their own backyard."

Rockwell glanced out the window, shocked at how close they were to the people searching for them. "Are you insane? How could you pick a place so close to the cops?"

"Relax," Crowley said. "They'd never think to look

for us only a block or two from one of their own facilities. They're too busy running around Albany." He tapped an index finger against his temple. "And we ain't there. Pure genius. Like hiding right out in the open."

Zacarelli eased the blanket back just enough to get another look at the sheriff's facility. He was convinced more than ever that Crowley was out of his mind, taking insane chances.

"Drop that cover!" Crowley snapped. Zacarelli immediately released his grip allowing the blanket to fall back in place over the window. Crowley's flashlight beam swept across the dusty room. "Make yourself comfortable." He had his sleeping bag laid out on the floor. There were two more rolled up in the corner along with a box filled with canned food, snacks, and bottles of water. "Bathroom's in there," he said, pointing his flashlight toward a doorway on the far wall.

Rockwell dropped his package to the floor causing a puff of dust to rise up. He and Zacarelli shuffled across the darkened room. Every step they took elicited a creak from the aged floor. Stopping in front of the doorway, they saw nothing but darkness. Crowley came up behind the two men and pointed his flashlight through the doorway.

In the center of the room sat a wooden crate with a ragged hole about the diameter of a basketball knocked through its top. A red plastic bucket sat under the opening. A few rolls of toilet paper were within reach of the crate. The flashlight beam rested on the crate and bucket like a spotlight illuminating a stage.

"There's your shitter," Crowley announced.

"You're kidding, right?" Rockwell said.

"It's not fancy but it does the job. Just empty the bucket out the window." Rockwell looked at him like he was crazy. "You want regular plumbing then go check into a motel. Five minutes after you do the cops will be so far up your ass they'll be able to tickle your molars."

Rockwell and Zacarelli shuffled back to where Crowley had tossed the spare sleeping bags. They each grabbed one and unrolled it across from Crowley's. Phil Crowley was crouched over one of the boxes digging for something. He squatted down and placed a battery-powered lantern between the three of them. Flicking on the power switch, the three men were suddenly bathed in weak blue-tinged light. Crowley dropped onto his bag and unscrewed the cap from a bottle of water.

"Now, let's talk about tomorrow." Crowley tapped the map resting on the dusty floor in front of him. "Me and Tony will go over the route once more to make sure we're all set. In the meantime I've got my drone charging from a car battery in the other room."

"*Your* drone?" Rockwell said. "You mean *my* drone. Or at the very least, *our* drone."

Crowley pulled a pistol from the rear of his waistband and placed it in his lap. "I designed it. I built it. I'm flying it. So, yeah, it's my baby."

Zacarelli looked away, wanting no part of the exchange.

"Call it what you want," Rockwell said, "just as long as it gets the job done."

"Don't worry about me," Crowley said. "I know exactly what I have to do." He moved the pistol up by a pillow he had fashioned from some rolled up towels. With that confrontation over, Crowley took a long pull from a bottle of water, then said, "And while we're managing the drone strike, where will you be?"

"I'll be making sure the governor does not survive should there be any problem with *your* drone," Rockwell said.

Crowley stared at him, wanting nothing more than to go at Rockwell and take his rightful place as head of this operation. He nodded at Rockwell's package. "What's in there?"

Rockwell tugged at the string. The knot let loose and he pulled the paper off. Crowley and Zacarelli watched with interest as Rockwell laid out a new pair of dark blue jeans, a long-sleeved, light blue chambray shirt with CREW stitched above the left hand pocket, a highly-polished pair of new black shoes, and a navy-blue ball cap with gold lettering. "This is my backup plan," Rockwell said.

Zacarelli leaned in to get a better look at the lettering on the ball cap. It read, *USS SLATER DE-766.* Above the lettering was a profile of the old warship. "How is this your backup plan?"

"I had one of our loyal followers who still thinks this is all about staging a peaceful protest pick this stuff up for me. I plan to get aboard the ship where Clifton will be speaking by looking like one of the crew working the rally."

"And you think you can actually get through all the security around the ship?" Crowley asked.

"I did it before," Rockwell replied. "No reason I can't do it again. Especially if you two do your job with the fake IEDs."

"You got confidence. I'll give you that," Zacarelli said.

Rockwell turned to Crowley. "What about our weapons?"

"Just like we talked about. I'll have them ready for you in the morning."

"The last thing is the fake IEDs," Rockwell said.

Crowley moved the light closer to the Albany street map on the floor. "Tony and I will take the Taurus and place the IEDs around the city before daybreak. Clifton is scheduled to speak at noon so we'll make anonymous calls to the cops and start them running all over the place around 11:00 A.M. We have eight IEDs. We'll call in a new location every five minutes, always far from the previous location. They'll have no choice but to pull personnel away from the rally."

Zacarelli pointed at a number of spots on the map where they intended to hide the IEDs. "That should spread the cops out real wide and open up the net around the *Slater*."

"And after the drone strike?" Rockwell asked.

"We'll leave the van on the street and disappear in all the confusion," Crowley said. "I got another junker hidden close by. It'll be easy enough to get to and get the hell outta Dodge."

"What about you?" Zacarelli asked.

Rockwell gazed in silence at the battery-operated lantern at their feet. "Don't worry about me," he said, then held something up for the others to see. Crowley and Zacarelli leaned forward to get a better look at what dangled from Rockwell's hand. The weak illumination from the lantern bounced off a pair of military-style dog tags hanging from a chain. "The same person who got the clothes for me bought these custom-made dog tags from the USS *Slater*'s website." The tags read *Suzanne & Thomas Rockwell, RIP.*

"I plan to put these around Clifton's neck. Right before I kill her."

Chapter Forty
Albany, NY
July 4, 4:49 AM

The blue Taurus crept through the dark streets of Albany trying to beat the sunrise. Phil Crowley checked the rearview mirror, then pulled to the curb, easing to a stop under a streetlamp. Tony Zacarelli studied the map under the dim light.

"Looks like the next location is Dewey's Donut Shop." Zacarelli leaned forward. "One block straight up from here."

"How many is that?" Crowley asked.

Zacarelli took a quick look at the space behind his seat. They had eight IEDs in a tattered cardboard box on the floor when they began. "Two left." He retrieved one of the IEDs and settled back. "Ready when you are."

Crowley eased slowly onto Madison Avenue. Things were going well so far. They didn't need to be stopped by an overzealous cop for a minor traffic infraction.

The two men had spent the past hour crisscrossing the city. They followed the string of markings they had previously designated on their Albany street map. At each location, Zacarelli slipped out of the Taurus, hid one of the IEDs where it wouldn't be found until they called in their anonymous tip to the police, then jumped back into the car. Crowley had decided to add his own message to each device. *A BIG BOOM FOR GOV. CLIFTON* was scrawled in large black letters on every one of the fake pipe bombs.

* * *

Nine minutes later, Zacarelli hopped into the car and Crowley pulled away from a downtown college campus. "That's all eight." Zacarelli glanced over his shoulder to make sure no one was following them. "We did it, man. We actually did it!"

"Don't get too cocky," Crowley said. "This was the easy part. We still gotta launch the drone."

"Yeah, right." Zacarelli tapped on the dashboard. "We'll be okay though, right?"

"Just stick to the route I laid out for you and follow my orders. We'll be outta this damn city before nightfall." Crowley stared straight ahead. "And with a shitload of cash in our pockets."

"I hope so."

Rockwell's final payoff to Crowley and Zacarelli had taken a last minute twist. He would not tell them where their cash was located until he saw the drone approaching the *Slater*. At that point he would call Crowley and give him the pickup location. The three men had argued at great length. Crowley and Zacarelli feared they wouldn't be able to get to their monetary getaway cache, but finally gave up when it became clear that Rockwell would not yield. Evidently he did not believe in the old adage that there was honor among thieves, or in this case, among murderers.

The blue Taurus crossed the Troy-Menands Bridge

and once again buried itself in the bushes under the low trees behind South End Tavern. Crowley and Zacarelli hurried into the vacant restaurant. Moments later, they carried the drone and controller out with Rockwell's assistance and carefully put them in the back of the old white van. Like cockroaches disappearing when the kitchen lights come on, Rockwell, Crowley, and Zacarelli rushed back into the dark building as the sun crept over the horizon.

Chapter Forty-One
Albany, NY
July 4, 10:33 AM

The day was shaping up to be a beauty. Bright sun, blue sky, very few clouds, and no humidity. This was the type of day that crowds of supporters and the news media loved when it came to making big political announcements. Clifton must have a fix in with the angels.

The sun felt warm on my face as I waited in line next to the police van marked with a big number two on its side. I watched as personnel received their tablets, trackers, and radio gear. After verifying everything was working correctly, they were quickly ushered to small shuttle vehicles that whisked them away. Next stop—the area around the USS *Slater*. From there they would head to their assigned posts.

"Name?"

I swung my attention to the open side door of the police van. There stood the same pair of IT wunderkinds that I had dealt with last night.

"Rick Patterson."

IT gal checked her tablet. "ID, please, Mr. Patterson."

I flipped my wallet open and flashed my PI creds. IT gal tapped her screen. I couldn't help but wonder if anyone used a clipboard and paper anymore. She announced my name to IT guy. He retrieved the black zipper case containing my tablet and tracker from the previous evening and opened it. IT gal then rattled off a string of numbers which IT guy verified. He activated my devices.

While IT guy pointed out a few things on my tablet screen, IT gal was speaking on her headset. "Activating tracker alpha zero niner three one dash two seven. Name: Patterson, Rick. Security consultant with APD."

A small blue box appeared on my screen. My name, along with the other information that IT gal had recited, appeared. IT gal spoke into her headset again. "Confirmed." IT guy handed me my tracker and watched as I clipped it to the left side of my belt. With a Velcro strap, he secured the tablet to my left inner arm just above my wrist. Finally, he gave me a radio which I clipped onto the right side of my belt. I was glad I had decided to use my shoulder holster instead of the one that clipped to my belt. One more device and my trousers might have fallen down.

A police cadet led me to one of the shuttles, then turned and headed back to the line of numbered police vans. "Close the door," said the driver. "You're the last one for this run." I squeezed in with the mixed bag of personnel and slid the door closed. I was on my way.

* * *

It only took a few minutes to get from the numbered police vans lining the Washington Avenue side of Albany's West Capitol Park to where the *Slater* was moored. The APD had done a pretty good job of keeping the area clear and traffic moving.

I stepped from the van and checked my tablet. A gold X blinked on the screen up by the bow of the warship. The IT kids had instructed us that the gold X was the COPPS system telling us where we were supposed to be, so off I went, chasing it on my screen. Sure enough, it led me right to the dock by the bow of the ship.

I checked my watch. It was almost 11:00 o'clock. There wasn't much going on where I was stationed but I had a feeling that would soon change as I observed news vans of every shape, size, and color beginning to line the street that ran next to the *Slater*'s dock. They were laying out cables as thick as my arm, and an entire forest of antenna masts was being raised.

Nearby, a cluster of men and women raced across the forward gangway carrying snacks, refreshments, and handouts from a constant stream of delivery vans along with crates, ropes, and other items I couldn't identify. I had been informed that they were volunteers who worked aboard the *Slater*. All were dressed in dark blue jeans, long-sleeved light blue chambray shirts with CREW stitched above the left pocket, highly-polished black shoes, and navy-blue ball caps with a reproduction of the *Slater* in gold. Many similarly clad volunteers scampered all over the old warship. Two were performing quite a balancing act in an attempt to hang red, white, and blue bunting from the port side of the ship's flying bridge where Governor Clifton would give her speech.

I took a quick look at the news vans behind me. Seeing all the cameras prompted me to give myself a once over to make sure I had properly met the dress requirements for the job. I wore a white shirt, black trousers, navy-blue jacket, and matching ball cap. *APD Security* in bright yellow lettering appeared over the left side of my chest, across my back in larger lettering, and on the front of the ball cap. Maybe I wouldn't make the cover of *GQ* but there was no doubt I was there to work security.

There was a shortage of new radio equipment so I was one of the guys who had been given an old style handheld from the surplus stock of electronics. Removing the radio from my belt, I adjusted the volume and performed a radio check. After receiving a response, I clipped the radio back onto my belt and stood with my back to the *Slater*. I scanned the mass of newspeople, wondering if my friend Beth from the local all-news television station would be here. She had really saved the day for Kyle and me by letting us go through all the news footage. If she hadn't accommodated us, I'm not sure we would have found Gregory Rockwell's picture. And where would we be then?

That made me think about Rockwell and the two maniacs he was working with. Where had they disappeared to? It was as if they had dropped out of sight. Maybe they got smart and left the area. The old warship floated serenely behind me, a growing crowd of spectators bellying up to the barricades. Maybe the bombers weren't that smart and still lurked in Albany. A chill ran through me. They could even be in the crowd just out of sight.

A black town car bracketed by large black SUVs pulled up to the dock. The police held the cheering crowd back as Governor Helen Clifton, dressed in one of her trademark sky-blue business suits, exited the limo. A wedge of New York State Troopers split the crowd, opening a path for Governor Clifton. Andy Kohler trailed behind her as they traversed the gangway and disappeared into the *Slater*.

It was showtime.

Chapter Forty-Two
USS *Slater* (DE-766)
Albany, NY
July 4, 11:20 AM

Damn. This was number five.

I watched as a pair of APD officers dashed to their patrol car in the parking area next to the USS *Slater*. A second later the car tore out of the lot, lights flashing, sirens blaring, tires squealing. They were being dispatched to the latest bomb threat. That made five so far around the city.

I heard the first call come in over my radio at 11:00 o'clock. The second about five minutes later, and the third, fourth, and fifth at around five-minute intervals. You didn't have to be a genius to think that somebody might be orchestrating this whole thing according to a well-planned timetable. The question was who and why. And was it a coincidence that it was happening on Governor Clifton's big day or was it connected?

Officers not assigned to security around the *Slater* handled the first three calls. The last two calls drew from *Slater*'s security contingent, knocking our number of APD officers down by four. It looked like the officers patrolling the city suddenly had more work than they could handle. If this kept up we might lose a few troopers and fire personnel along with more APD officers. Maybe even a Homeland Security or FBI agent. For a brief moment I wondered if Rockwell and his two pals had resurfaced and were responsible for this sudden epidemic of IEDs.

* * *

Bomb threat number six squawked from my radio. I checked my watch. It was 11:27. A little over five minutes since the last threat was called in. I heard shouting and saw two more troopers jump into their car. The engine roared to life and the blue-and-gold New York State Trooper vehicle rocketed from the parking area. Our numbers were now down by six.

The tablet strapped to my arm began to beep. I studied the screen. Two gray blocks disappeared. Those had to be the two troopers who had just left the area. Moments ago two pairs of blue blocks representing the APD officers responding to bomb threats four and five had winked out. Now, a gold X popped up near the forward gangway leading onto the *Slater*. The system was assigning me to a new position to take up the slack. I chased the X as a number of other colored blocks moved around the screen like a video game gone nuts. It looked like the COPPS system was getting one hell of a field test.

As I arrived at the gangway, the gold X on my screen disappeared, replaced by a blue block with my name in it. Two APD officers, one female, one male, were already positioned there. I opened my mouth to speak but before I got a word out, the female's tablet beeped. She held up her index finger while she checked the screen. "Looks like I'm being shifted onto the rear deck."

"I've just been reassigned to this location," I said.

With a nod, the officer turned and pounded across the gangway. She veered toward the rear of the warship and disappeared from view. The officer standing with me, a rugged-looking, middle-aged man I'd never met before, held a tablet computer displaying a list of names. He extended his hand. "Name's Cowan."

"Rick Patterson."

"Hell of a day already," Cowan said.

"Yeah, hell of a week, actually."

I still had this nagging feeling that Rockwell and his buddies could be involved in what was happening around the city. It was too much of a coincidence. And if they were beyond the barricades watching and waiting to make another move on the *Slater*, there would be no way in hell to pick them out. The crowd was growing rapidly and security was shrinking just as rapidly. Not a good formula for success. I wondered if I was the only one who thought these guys could be connected. Maybe they should run it past the great and powerful COPPS.

As we stood at the end of the gangway, a black Suburban pulled up. An older man exited the vehicle. An assorted mob of men and women streamed out of the vehicle and surrounded him. The knot of people moved toward us. When he got closer I realized it was the senior United States senator from New York. The only reason I recognized him was because he had been heavy in the news for the past year trying to pass legislation having to do with drones. I couldn't recall his name but I did remember that the news media referred to him as Senator Drone-Killer. From what I recalled, the stories said he was bent on outlawing drones. To his credit there were reports popping up every day about hobbyists and kids and John Q. Publics flying homemade drones around airports, sports arenas, and other places where they shouldn't be, causing all kinds of chaos. Not to mention lobbyists of big business trying to get approval for delivering consumer products via drones. The friendly skies were getting very crowded with this new technology.

Cowan leaned over and whispered, "I'll check them in. You just stand there and look official."

The senator stopped before us, a smile spreading across his face as he looked around. When he saw there were no cameras on him yet, his smile faded.

"Greetings, Senator," Cowan said. He ticked the box before the senator's name on his tablet. "You may proceed, sir."

The senator turned to me as he stepped onto the gangway and gripped the wobbly railing. Not sure what I was supposed to say, but feeling like he expected me to say something, I blurted out, "Welcome aboard, sir."

"Thank you, young man." The senator threw me a mock salute before starting across the gangway. An APD officer and two volunteers in crew garb waited at the other end to meet him. Cowan checked the rest of the senator's entourage one by one. When the last member of the senator's party had crossed onto the *Slater*, Cowan smirked.

"Welcome aboard?" he said, shaking his head. I cracked a smile and shrugged, but I felt my face grow hot. Cowan rolled his eyes.

A string of local politicians approached us to get on the warship. They were followed by Governor Clifton's two personal photographers and a videographer. Given that there was a limited amount of space on the forward and aft decks, there would not be many more guests crossing the gangway onto the ship.

Our radios suddenly came alive with the code for

another bomb threat. That made seven. This had gone beyond insane. Cowan and I watched two more gray blocks disappear from our tablets as COPPS dispatched a pair of troopers to check out the latest call. We were down by eight as another trooper vehicle sped from the parking area.

* * *

At 11:38 another bomb threat came in. Number eight. No doubt about it—they were definitely coming in every five minutes, give or take. Two more colored blocks around the *Slater* disappeared. Our security force was down by ten. How long could this go on before they cancelled the event?

I stood at my post with Cowan at the entrance to the gangway. We sweated out the next five minutes checking people aboard the *Slater* as we waited for another bomb threat. Volunteer crew members continued to rush back and forth across the gangway like ants on speed. After repeatedly eyeballing their IDs we began to let them pass without stopping them.

Everyone remained glued to their radios but IED number nine never materialized. Another five minutes dragged by. Cowan gave a sigh of relief. Maybe the assault had ended.

"Think it's over?" I asked.

"Maybe." Cowan's tone didn't fill me with confidence. He thumbed his cap back on his head, his eyes sweeping across the burgeoning mass behind the barricades. "Question is, what's next?"

It was a fair question, but one I didn't want to think about. None of the IEDs had actually exploded so maybe the worst really was over.

A high-pitched squeal erupted, shattering the carnival-like atmosphere around the warship. The racket stopped everyone in their tracks; the area around the dock looked like it was filled with mannequins.

My eyes locked on the flying bridge far above us. My pounding heart slowed as I realized it was only the sound system being powered up and adjusted. Feeling foolish for being so jumpy, I snuck a glance at Cowan to see if he had noticed my abysmal reaction. To my surprise, the APD officer was hunkered down, his hand resting on his holstered Beretta. I guess I wasn't alone in being on edge. It even crossed my mind that maybe no one would have minded if I shot the sound guy for scaring the crap out of us all.

I checked my watch. It was 11:51. Governor Clifton was scheduled to arrive at noon.

Chapter Forty-Three
USS *Slater* (DE-766)
Albany, NY
July 4, 11:51 AM

The blast of noise washed over the volunteer crew members like an aural tsunami. They froze in place, all eyes riveted on the flying bridge of the USS *Slater*, everyone holding their breath. Nestled quietly among them was a well-disguised, and also startled, Gregory Rockwell. As soon as the realization hit that it was only the sound system being powered up, the volunteers came back to life, and resumed ferrying supplies to the old warship.

Rockwell had patiently spent the previous seventy-eight minutes unseen in the shadows of a nearby building, waiting for the perfect opportunity to sneak aboard the USS *Slater*. His persistence paid off as he observed a pack of similarly clothed volunteer crew members walking along the sidewalk approaching the warship's dock.

Extracting himself from the shadows, he stealthily caught up and fell in behind them, then inserted himself into the excited group. Hidden behind dark aviator-style sunglasses with his ball cap pulled down almost to the bridge of his nose, Rockwell slapped a couple of backs, high-fived a few hands, and acted like he had spent time with them. Even though they didn't know him, they were too embarrassed to say so. By the time they arrived at the dock he had convinced them he was one of the gang. With his face clean-shaven and his hair trimmed short, he blended right in with the group of volunteers.

Rockwell's eyes fell upon the laminated ID tags on blue lanyards around their necks. That was the one part of his disguise that was missing. He hoped no one would notice. It only took three seconds for his hope to be dashed.

"Where's your ID?" an attractive twenty-something female asked him. A laminated tag identified her as Lisa Galloway. "You need an ID to get aboard."

Years lost wandering the roads of America had transformed Gregory Rockwell from a young man with a bright future into a broken man with nothing to live for. And somewhere along the way he learned to be cruel and cunning, crafting a lie as easily as some would draw a breath. Right now he needed to sell himself as an absent-minded patriot.

Like a chameleon, he plastered a lop-sided grin on his face and said to Lisa, "It's right here." A look of horror crossed his features as he patted his chest, found nothing, then scanned the concrete dock around him. "It was around my neck! Oh, geez! Where the heck is it?" He jerked his head from side to side. "I lost it! I can't believe I lost it!" He held his head in his hands as the others now stared at his Oscar-winning performance. He looked like he was about to cry. "What am I supposed to do now?"

"Calm down," Lisa said. "We'll just give your name to the security guys watching the gangway. You have other ID on you, right?"

It was time for act two of Rockwell's performance; he patted his jeans pockets, looking more alarmed than before. He was really going to have to sell this until he came up with a better plan. "Yeah, I...oh, no. I must have forgotten my wallet when I rushed out this morning."

Lisa Galloway shrugged. " Can you run home and get some ID?"

Rockwell thought quickly. "I live too far away. I'll never make it back in time."

A young man who had been listening stepped up. "Can't we vouch for him?"

"You know him?" Lisa asked.

"I think I recognize him," Joe Alessio said, rubbing his chin. "He's...uh." Just as Alessio was about to admit he never saw him before, Rockwell broke in.

"I'm Buddy Driscoll," Rockwell said, throwing out the name of someone whose path he'd crossed years ago in Illinois. It hadn't ended well for the real Buddy Driscoll, but that was another story. "You remember me, right? I just joined up."

"Yeah, right," Alessio replied, not wanting to admit he didn't recognize one of their own. "You're Buddy." He turned to the other volunteers behind him. "You guys remember Buddy." A number of them followed Alessio's lead and nodded. No one wanted to look foolish, but soon they all would.

Like sheep being led to slaughter, Rockwell thought.

Rockwell's mantra for years had been never to draw attention to himself, either for something good or bad. He didn't need these fools marching him up to the two guards on the gangway and having their sole focus pinned on him. He was sure they had seen his picture, along with Crowley's and Zacarelli's, from the BOLO that had been issued. Even with a haircut and shave, a seasoned security person might recognize him. Rockwell refused to get tripped up this close to fulfilling his promise to his deceased parents.

"I think those guys are plenty busy right now," Rockwell said. "We shouldn't bother them with my stupid mistake. How about if I help carry things as far as the gangway and you guys take them aboard?"

"If you're sure," Alessio said.

"Yep," Rockwell replied. "That way I can at least do my part without causing a fuss."

Lisa Galloway tugged her ball cap down and shouted, "Okay, people. Let's get this stuff aboard!" Boxes were hoisted onto shoulders and hand trucks, everyone hustling toward the gangway.

The cell phone in the front pocket of Rockwell's jeans vibrated. He stepped away from the rest of the volunteers and checked the phone as soon as he was out of earshot. He had received a photograph. Rockwell expanded the image, shading the screen from the bright midday sun. He found himself looking at the back end of the white van Crowley and Zacarelli were using. The vehicle's rear doors were wide open showing the drone sitting atop its deadly payload. It was festooned with streamers and a banner, a slice of Albany's South End just visible past the doors. The text under the picture read:

In position. Ready to go. Time to pay up.
I launch when you send $$$ location.

Gregory Rockwell chewed on his lower lip. Realizing he had no choice but to trust Crowley this one last time, Rockwell typed the location of the final payoff:

Boarding house room. Under floorboards. Far right corner.

He hesitated before sending his response. This was a true leap of faith given Crowley's character. He reluctantly pressed SEND.

Rockwell gazed up at the clear blue sky. Any minute now the drone should circle the USS *Slater*. Soon after that, if all went well, the flying bridge where Governor Helen Clifton was spouting her lies would be awash in flames and his debt to his mother and father would be paid. He felt the cold body of the automatic pistol tucked into the waistband in the small of his back and covered by his shirttail. It was his insurance just in case things didn't go according to plan. All he had to do was find a way to sneak himself and his pistol aboard the warship.

* * *

Rockwell hoofed boxes of T-shirts emblazoned with the likeness of the USS *Slater*, booklets detailing the history of the warship, and other souvenirs to the entrance to the gangway where he handed them off to legitimate volunteer crew members, always careful to keep his head down. Rockwell took note that the two men forming a defensive line preventing unauthorized access to the warship had stopped using their handheld metal detector on the group of volunteers who kept ferrying items onto the ship. They must have figured checking them once was good enough. And that might be his way aboard if he timed it right.

Rockwell's attention was suddenly snagged by a loud noise like a muted buzzsaw. A white dirigible, approximately twelve feet long out over the water, slowly approached the ship's tall mast. He shaded his eyes. The name of a local bank filled its flanks. He could just make out two small, whirling fans, one on either side of a tiny fake passenger compartment hanging below the dirigible's body. Whoever was at the controls was doing a good job staying the course in the light breeze. The airship crept over the dock and looked like it was getting ready to circle the warship.

Rockwell got back to moving items to the gangway. The pile was almost gone and he still had no idea how he was going to get aboard. The two men guarding the gangway had not had any reason to ask for his ID or wand him yet, but they certainly would if he made a move to get on the ship.

Screams, cheers, and wild applause erupted from the crowd. Rockwell gazed at the flying bridge, a box of metal replicas of the USS *Slater* clutched in his hands. Governor Helen Clifton stood waving at the crowd and smiling in all her glory before her adoring crowd. Through slitted eyes filled with hate, Rockwell saw her as the reason his parents were dead and his life was nothing more than a series of useless years leading to this day, a day that he probably would not live to see the end of.

The mass of spectators behind the barricades began to yell and point toward the USS *Slater*. Rockwell's head jerked upwards as he heard the two fans powering the dirigible overhead whining at an impossibly high speed. He watched in fascination as a gust of wind grabbed the tiny airship and propelled it toward the flying bridge like a fat torpedo aimed right for Helen Clifton. When Clifton's entourage realized the dirigible was on a collision course with the flying bridge, they hustled her back from the edge of the exposed platform.

To Rockwell's delight, most of the law enforcement personnel on the dock and warship stood, eyes transfixed, on the runaway airship. The volunteer crew members froze on the gangway, their cell phones out, competing to record the impending disaster.

Seizing the moment of confusion, Rockwell used the box he had been holding to shield his face and sprinted for the gangway. He zipped unseen past the security guard and the APD officer and shouldered his way through the volunteers lining the gangway. As soon as his feet hit the deck of the *Slater*, he tossed the box aside and dove through the first open hatchway he came upon.

Chapter Forty-Four
USS *Slater* (DE-766)
Albany, NY
July 4, 12:17 PM

I watched in horror as the crowd behind the barricades became a mob, thrusting forward like a tidal wave, smartphones clutched high over their heads, everyone trying to get that perfect disaster video for the internet. The wood barricades holding them back from the USS *Slater* collapsed and people spilled onto the dock, the mass spreading toward the warship. Spreading toward me.

Someone rushed by behind me and raced across the gangway. He shoved his fellow volunteers to the point where a few almost went over the side into the slot of water between the dock and warship. I figured he was running from the crowd out of fear, seeking safety on the ship.

I caught a glimpse of his face as he hit the deck of the *Slater*, tossed the box he'd been carrying, and disappeared through an open hatch. I tried to convince myself I hadn't seen who I was sure I just had seen. It could have been the angle of the runner's body or the way the sunlight hit his face. Perhaps it was a subconscious suggestion from somewhere at the back of my mind. No. It wasn't any of those. I was damn positive I had just seen Gregory Rockwell, kidnapper and attempted bomber, get on the ship.

"Cowan! Cowan!" I yelled over my shoulder as I pushed my way onto the gangway. My partner had abandoned his post to help corral the crowd that had trampled over the barricades. He became part of a long line of blue and gray uniforms forming a pitiful human barrier against the surging crowd. I was on my own.

I yanked the radio off my belt, pressed the transmit key, and opened my mouth to report what I'd just seen. Before I could utter one sound, two volunteer crew members collided with me. I stared helplessly over the edge of the gangway as my radio went sailing out of my hand and splashed into the water below.

Realizing I had no choice but to run Rockwell down on my own, I charged over the gangway like an all-star running back, sprinting through every gap between the volunteers clogging my path.

When I hit the *Slater*'s deck I stopped to check the small tablet still strapped to my forearm. I didn't recall any way to send a message. Colored blocks moved all over the screen, their paths crisscrossing each other and coming together in a line between the *Slater* and where I assumed the barricades used to stand. If COPPS had an actual brain, it would probably be exploding right about now.

The only thing I could be sure of was that Rockwell would have to make his way up toward the flying bridge if his target was the governor. I mentally crossed my fingers and took off for the hatch I had seen Rockwell vanish through.

* * *

The chaos on the USS *Slater*'s dock subsided as quickly as it had erupted. The spectators clogging the pier cheered loudly as the gust of wind suddenly died and the runaway airship sailed harmlessly past the flying bridge, mere inches from where Governor Helen Clifton had begun her monumental speech just moments ago.

Governor Clifton huddled near the base of the *Slater*'s mast. She was flanked by her videographer and one of her personal photographers, and shielded by Andy Kohler and APD Lieutenant Larry Dawson. Since space on the flying bridge was limited, the senior United States senator from New York and Albany's mayor were relegated to standing below on the bow. Neither looked happy about being so far away from the cameras.

Dawson blew out a breath as he watched the airship crawl by without touching them. He grabbed his radio. "This is Dawson. Find out who's controlling that blimp and get it the hell out of the *Slater*'s airspace!" He released the transmit button, thought a second, then pressed it again. "Dawson again. I want the airspace around the *Slater* declared off-limits as of right now." As soon as he received confirmation, he turned to Kohler. "It's safe to go back out whenever the governor is ready."

Before Kohler could speak, Clifton charged back out to the flying bridge with her photographer and videographer in tow and gazed out over the undulating crowd covering the dock. As she waved like a conquering hero, the crowd went wild cheering.

Kohler gave Dawson a barely-disguised shrug. "Guess she's ready." He followed Clifton out and took up position behind her.

Helen Clifton took a backseat to no one. Never did,

never would. It was ingrained in her DNA. Her supporters loved it, her opponents feared it. She had a plaque on her office wall that offered perfect insight into her character. It read, *In battle, if you are not attacking, you are retreating.* And Helen Clifton never retreated.

The crowd grew silent as Clifton tapped the microphone with a well-manicured fingernail. The muffled boom-boom-boom told her it was still on. "It appears there are those who will stop at nothing to keep me from speaking the truth. They have to do better than a big old gas bag to shut me up!" The crowd whooped and cheered, "Helen! Helen! Helen!" Clifton had them under her spell. Now was the perfect time to declare her run for President of the United States.

As Clifton launched into her announcement, Dawson's attention was drawn to three people wrestling with the dirigible in the nearby parking lot. He stepped away from the governor and spoke softly into his radio. "This is Dawson. Somebody make sure those idiots in the parking area do not launch that dirigible again." He then checked his tablet. He was the only security person aboard the *Slater*. "And get our people back to their assigned positions." As soon as his message was acknowledged, he checked the tablet again. One blue block moved onto the ship. He checked the ID. It belonged to Rick Patterson. *Patterson is assigned to watch the gangway. Where the hell is he going?*

* * *

Gregory Rockwell darted through the open hatch on the main deck. He rushed through the narrow passageways, feeling like a confused mouse in a tight maze. He had checked the detailed drawings of the various decks on the USS *Slater* website when he was deciding where to place the original knapsack bombs, but right now he was in such a fever pitch his mind was blank.

Metal boxes covered in lights, dials, and switches filled every available space. Thick cables and wires snaked all along the overhead and climbed the bulkheads like tangled jungle vines. There seemed to be no order to any of the areas he passed through.

Rockwell found the metal ladder leading to the deck above him. A sign indicated it was called the superstructure. He couldn't remember exactly how far up he had to go until he got to the deck where Clifton was speaking. All he knew was that he had to keep moving up, higher and higher, until there were no more ladders. He thought how fitting it was that he would be making his last stand at the pinnacle of the warship.

Rockwell searched the superstructure for the way up to the next deck. He found another sign pointing to a ladder leading to what was called the navigating bridge. As he moved from deck to deck, he could hear Clifton's muffled voice punctuated by repeated bouts of cheering from her faithful sheep packing the dock. Rockwell launched himself up the ladder, surprised he had yet to run into any volunteer crew members or security people. It was as if the ship was abandoned.

He stepped warily onto the navigating bridge, surveyed the small room, then crept to the ladder leading up to the flying bridge. That's where Clifton would be speaking to her followers. The hatch was open. Rockwell paused at the foot of the ladder, his sweaty hands gripping the railings. The open hatch was all that separated him from redemption.

A warm breeze blew through the opening, spilled down the ladder, and washed over him. He squinted up at the brilliant blue sky. Clifton's voice was louder than ever as was the roar of the crowd on the dock below. Rockwell took a deep breath and crept up the metal ladder. He stopped halfway to pull the automatic pistol from the rear of his waistband, stared at it for a long moment, then edged toward the open hatch. The end of his heartbreaking odyssey was near.

Chapter Forty-Five
South End Neighborhood
Albany, NY
July 4, 12:24 PM

Zacarelli sped down Dongan Avenue in Albany's South End, not entirely sure where he was going. They were running late and Zacarelli was panicking. They should have been in position by now with the drone in the air. He was driving the old white van too fast, too erratically, and Crowley yelling at him only made matters worse. The map of traffic detours they had so painstakingly detailed on their dry run was now useless. The crowds had swelled so far beyond APD estimates that the police department instituted a lot of last minute traffic changes for Albany's South End neighborhood.

"There!" Crowley barked from the passenger seat. "Take that street!"

Zacarelli stomped on the brakes and yanked the wheel hard to the right. The van skidded sideways onto John Street, his maneuver almost taking down a black lamp post at the corner.

"Slow down, you moron! You're gonna wreck the

drone if you don't get us killed first!"

"I'm doin' the goddamn best I can!" Zacarelli said, eyes on the narrow one-lane street in front of him.

"Pull over here." Crowley pointed to a derelict church. "Get right up there next to the stairs."

The van jumped the curb, the steering wheel almost spinning out of Zacarelli's sweaty hands. They drove across the cracked concrete sidewalk and through eight feet of dead grass, coming to a stop next to a buckled set of rusty iron steps leading up to a plywood-covered entryway.

"Hurry up," Crowley said. "We gotta get inside and launch the drone."

The two men opened the rear doors of the vehicle and lifted the over-sized drone out. "Grab that crowbar," Crowley said as he slipped a knapsack containing the controller and two pistols over his shoulder.

Zacarelli glanced up at the tall building. The old stone structure took up the entire block and looked more like a medieval fortress than a former house of worship. Most of the stained glass windows were busted out and pieces of weathered plywood covered the entryways. Patches of shingles were missing from the roof and green ivy engulfed the lower half of the tall outer walls.

"Is this place safe?" he asked.

"It's safe enough for what we have to do," Crowley said. "Now pry it open."

Zacarelli rested his end of the drone on the metal handrail and inserted the end of the crowbar under the edge of the plywood sheet blocking their way. It came away with little effort. They hastened inside and rested the drone on the dirty floor, where pigeon droppings and rodent feces covered the old stone tiles.

"Get that plywood back in place before someone

sees us," Crowley said. Zacarelli did as he was told. When he turned back Crowley was tucking a pistol in the rear of his waistband.

"Where's mine?"

Crowley reached into the knapsack and withdrew the second pistol. "Sure you know how to handle one of these?"

"Just give it to me." Crowley tossed it to him. Zacarelli caught the weapon, ejected and checked the magazine, then rammed it back in. He couldn't wait to get his cash and be done with this arrogant bastard. He slipped the weapon into his waistband.

Crowley pointed over Zacarelli's head. "We're going up to that loft by those windows. That's where we set the drone loose." They lifted the drone and made their way up the rickety wooden stairs that creaked with every step. The empty window frames in the second-story choir loft looked out on Interstate 787. The dock where the USS *Slater* rested was on the other side of the raised interstate.

Crowley ordered Zacarelli to keep watch out the window frame to make sure they were clear. He checked over the drone and armed the IED snuggled beneath it. Crowley pulled the controller from the knapsack. The eight small black propellers began to spin faster and faster until they became shimmering discs. The drone lifted slowly off the floor, throwing out a wave of dust in all directions. The buzzing of the small motors powering the drone filled the room.

Zacarelli approached the window frame. He searched outside, saw no one, and gave Crowley a thumbs up. The drone edged closer to the window. It stopped in front of the opening, then eased through. Zacarelli lifted the banner and streamers so they would not get snagged. Once through the window frame, Crowley increased power. The drone charged forward sailing up over the raised interstate and disappeared from view as it dropped over the far side.

"Move the van down the street and hide it," Crowley said. With his eyes on the controller screen, he grinned like a hungry wolf spying a lost sheep. Zacarelli peered over Crowley's shoulder.

The USS *Slater* sat dead center on the controller's screen.

Chapter Forty-Six
USS *Slater* (DE-766)
Albany, NY
July 4, 12:29 PM

I slipped through the same open hatch on the main deck where I swore I'd seen Rockwell disappear. Sweeping the large room and seeing no one there, I made my way to a set of steps leading up to the next deck. A small sign let me know that in the Navy, stairs were called ladders. That would have to be trivia for another day. Right now, I needed to see if I had deserted my post for a legitimate reason. If I was wrong, my first big break in the PI business would quickly turn into my first big flop. Maybe my biggest and final flop.

I continued up the steps, or should I say ladder, and emerged onto the superstructure. Turning to my right, I saw the next ladder leading up. There were also a couple of doors, all painted dark gray.

Did I need to check each room for Rockwell or was he already above me? I never thought to check the individual rooms on the deck I'd just left. Too late now. I decided to err on the side of caution. I crept to the first door. A wall plate identified it as the Radio Room. The room was empty. Softly closing the door, I moved to the remaining pair of rooms marked Captain's Wardroom and Ship's Office. Both were empty.

I inched up the ladder leading to the next deck, carefully raising my head into the navigating bridge. The space was vacant. Three more gray doors marked CIC (Combat Information Center), Sea Cabin, and Steering Station. Three more empty rooms.

Maybe I was wrong and only imagined I'd seen Rockwell. I wondered if I should get back to my post by the gangway before I was missed. I checked the tablet on my forearm; blue and gray blocks were breaking away from the line holding the crowd back, probably returning to their assigned positions. I saw my own identifier over the *Slater.* Damn, COPPS had me dead to rights. It knew I was not where I had been ordered to be. I wondered if it would cut me some slack or blow the whistle on me. I had my answer as my identifier began to flash, then a yellow dashed line appeared, starting at my current position and marching all the way back to the end of the gangway. The damn computer had ratted me out.

I stood before the ladder leading down and froze. The space had suddenly gotten brighter, Clifton's voice louder. I glanced over my shoulder, and saw a second ladder leading to the next deck above me. Glaring sunlight poured through the open hatch. The silhouette of a figure crouched at the top, haloed by the light. He was leaning out. I moved to my left. When the figure blocked the sun, I saw Gregory Rockwell, gun in hand, looking like he was about to spring out of the hatch.

I reached inside my jacket, released the strap securing my pistol, then slid it out of its holster. The smooth metal made a barely audible hiss as it slid along the leather holster. In the silence, it sounded like a screaming heavy metal band. I brought my pistol up and leaned away from the foot of the ladder, figuring he would have a less direct shot at me.

"Hey!" I shouted. Rockwell snapped around, bringing his weapon up. "Drop the gun!" My fear had been that he would be so surprised that he would take a shot at me, but instead he sized me up, then kept moving. "C'mon, man," I pleaded. "Just put the gun down." His eyes narrowed into slits as he backed out through the hatch, using his butt to push it open. I was momentarily blinded by the light. Lowering my pistol, I retreated from the foot of the ladder.

I stood still until the red circles disappeared from my vision, then edged forward to peek up the ladder. The hatch was open and Rockwell was gone. I heard Governor Clifton stop speaking, then screams exploded from the crowd.

My eyes were riveted on the open hatch before me. It felt like I was looking through the gates of hell. One-way gates inviting me to my death. Without warning, I was back in that dark alley five years ago with Dave Taylor's blood all over me. All my doubts and fears about that night were back, engulfing me, threatening to suffocate me.

My body trembled and my gun felt like it weighed a ton. I swallowed hard, slammed my eyes shut, and tried to get myself under control. My heart was doing its damnedest to pound its way out of my heaving chest.

If I didn't respond to COPPS telling me where to go, surely the cavalry would show up to look for me. All I had to do was keep Rockwell from doing something stupid until help arrived— and not get killed in the effort.

Opening my eyes, I cautiously ascended the ladder

toward the open hatch. I held my gun at eye level, my hands thankfully steady again. Halfway up I could hear Rockwell screaming something about his parents to the governor, then yelling at Dawson that he better not move. If security personnel didn't know what was happening before, they surely did now. It was playing out in front of them; the bad guy and the victims giving the performances of their lifetimes on an elevated stage before the world.

I crouched at the threshold of the hatch. *Will this be the moment of my redemption or the day I die?* I heard Dave Taylor's voice in the recesses of my mind saying, Don't overthink the situation, Patterson. *Gotcha, Dave.* I took a deep breath and eased through the opening.

Chapter Forty-Seven
South End Neighborhood
Albany, NY
July 4, 12:36 PM

Zacarelli made his way down from the choir loft of the vacant church. The tired old staircase protested with every step, the continual creaking echoing off the cold stone walls of the empty structure. Crowley wanted him to move the van to a spot where it wouldn't be noticed. Arriving at the foot of the stairs, he could still hear Crowley up in the loft talking to himself, cheering on the drone like it was alive.

Zacarelli wanted to stash the van and get back up to the loft in time to see the explosion over the top of the interstate. After that, they would race back to Rockwell's boarding house to retrieve the hidden bag containing their payoff. And after that, goodbye Albany, and goodbye psycho Crowley.

He got to the entryway and pushed against the gray, warped plywood blocking his path. After initially lugging the drone inside, Zacarelli had secured the weathered barrier by pounding a few of the nails back into the doorframe with his fist.

Rather than yank the plywood down again, he pushed one side of it out, the old material bending but not breaking, then squeezed through the narrow slit between the plywood and the doorframe. The whoop-whoop of a siren startled him. He froze half in, half out, staring at a police car as it stopped at the curb across from the entryway.

The passenger window slid down exposing a blond-haired officer. "Hey! What the hell are you doing in there?"

Zacarelli was stunned. He had no idea what to say, instead staring silently back at the APD car, his mouth wide open. He could not reach his pistol. And if he could was he really prepared for a shootout? He tried to back into the church and found he was jammed. He couldn't go back, he couldn't go forward. He was a bug pinned to a display board.

"I'm talking to you!" the officer said. Zacarelli remained silent, still squirming to get back inside. The officer opened his door and got out. "You stay right there and keep your hands where I can see them!" Zacarelli caught a glimpse of the officer behind the wheel lifting a radio to his mouth.

Giving one final wholehearted shove, Zacarelli fell back inside the church, landing on his butt. The sheet of plywood snapped back over the entryway, but only for a second. No sooner had Zacarelli given a great sigh of relief than the plywood fell forward. It blocked the top of the twisted iron staircase but left the entryway wide open.

The officer stood at the bottom of the staircase, surprised and staring at him. Still on his butt, Zacarelli stared back at the officer. For a long moment neither moved, then the officer pointed at him. "Freeze! Do not move!" Zacarelli watched as the officer's hand hovered over his holstered pistol. That's all he needed to see. He rolled to his left across the dust and pigeon-feces-covered floor, whipping out his own pistol.

"Crowley!" Zacarelli screamed from the cover of the doorframe. "The cops are here! We're trapped!"

* * *

Crowley heard Zacarelli's warning loud and clear that the cops had arrived. He smiled recalling a quote he once heard from his time in the army. It was something about the best plan in the world going out the window as soon as the first bullet was fired. *Not this time*, he thought. He had planned ahead for this event.

It was time to put his failsafe plan into action. The drone had just arrived over the *Slater*. He caught a glimpse of Rockwell far below on the flying bridge, gun in hand, standing before the governor. He fired up a program enabling the drone to ignore the controller and autonomously circle the mast jutting up from the flying bridge. It would run that racetrack course five times before slamming into the red crosshairs he had just locked over the governor's head. As soon as a message came on the screen verifying his program was activated, he put the controller on the floor and stomped the crap out of it just to be on the safe side. Now no one could stop the drone from its mission.

Crowley yanked the pistol from his waistband, jacked the slide, and stood at the top of the stairs. "Get up here," he yelled down to Zacarelli.

* * *

"He's got a gun!" Officer Steve Flynn shouted as he dove around the corner of the vacant building. His partner, Dave Witkowski, had been standing outside the patrol car, the vehicle between him and the church. At

Flynn's warning, he dropped back into the car and called for assistance. Witkowski then slammed the vehicle door closed, dropped the shift lever into reverse, and floored the gas, sending the patrol car racing backwards. The car skidded to a halt blocking the road leading past the side of the church where Flynn was hiding. Witkowski exited the vehicle, using it as a shield, shouting to a growing crowd of curious rubberneckers to clear the area.

* * *

Zacarelli raced up the stairs and dove to the floor of the loft. Crowley had moved to a nearby window. He raised his leg and kicked a two-foot square piece of plywood from a window frame. As the wood sailed to the ground below them, he glanced out and saw the police car blocking the street.

"How many are out there?" he asked.

"Two," Zacarelli said. "One by the car. The other right outside the door." He began to wave his gun around. "What the hell are we supposed to do now?"

"Relax," Crowley said. "We're just gonna walk right out of here. There's two of them and two of us. We can take them." He turned away from the window to face Zacarelli, still on the floor. "But we gotta move right now before reinforcements arrive."

Zacarelli whipped his head back and forth like a crazy man. "No! They're gonna kill us. We gotta give up."

"You're either fighting your way out with me or *I'll* kill you right now. Your choice. You got three seconds."

"If we kill cops they'll—"

"One," Crowley said.

"This is insane—"

"Two." Crowley raised his pistol and trained it on Zacarelli cowering on the floor.

"Okay, goddamnit!" Zacarelli said. "Tell me what to

do."

"See?" Crowley said. "That wasn't so hard, was it?" Zacarelli reluctantly shook his head without uttering a word. "Go downstairs and watch the door. I'll be right down."

* * *

Steve Flynn waved to Dave Witkowski, then held up one finger. He saw Witkowski give him a thumbs up; he understood Flynn had seen only one person. Flynn leaned around the corner of the towering stone building so he could keep an eye on the entryway.

Flynn tried again to coax the man outside. "Throw your weapon out, then follow it with your hands on your head!" No reaction from inside. Flynn glanced at Witkowski. All his partner had for him was a shrug. Flynn yelled again. "Last chance! Throw your weapon out."

Flynn pulled back behind the corner of the building to wait for a reaction. If he had to sit there all day until reinforcements arrived, that was fine with him. He never claimed to be a hero.

* * *

Zacarelli crept down the stairs, trying to keep to the outside edges of each step to minimize the groaning from the old wood. He arrived at the foot of the stairs and tiptoed to the exposed entryway. Shafts of dusty sunlight splashed onto the worn wood floor, sending the shadows back into the old church. He edged to the left side of the opening, shielded by the ornately carved doorframe and waited for Crowley to join him.

Zacarelli heard the cop shouting at him to throw his gun out and give up. The cop sounded way too close. The creaking steps drew his attention. He watched Crowley descend the stairs. "What the hell?"

Crowley had donned a new set of clothes. He wore

old mismatched sneakers, a dirty blue plaid shirt, and ripped, filthy brown trousers topped with a worn-out, heavily stained coat and tattered baseball cap. As Crowley drew up behind him, Zacarelli saw he had rubbed dirt from the floor all over his face.

"What are you doing?" Zacarelli whispered.

Crowley grinned. "Getting out of here, just like I told you."

Crowley pointed out the doorway. Zacarelli turned to see what his partner was gesturing at. In a flash, Crowley brought his foot up to the middle of Zacarelli's back and shoved him from behind with everything he had. Zacarelli flew through the open doorway and slammed against the wrought iron railing of the steel stairs. He stood dumbfounded in plain view of the cops.

"No, wait! I—" Zacarelli raised his hands, forgetting about the gun he was still clutching.

Flynn popped out from behind the cover of the old church and let loose half a dozen rounds, then dropped back down. It was the first time he had ever fired his weapon on the job. He slipped to the ground, his back against the warm stone wall of the derelict church. He was too scared to get up to see if he had hit anything.

Zacarelli lurched drunkenly to the side of the stairs, then fell over the rail. He came to rest spread-eagled on his back, the pistol still clutched in his hand. To Flynn's credit, he scored on all six shots.

Dave Witkowski radioed that shots had been fired, then rushed to the man lying motionless on the dead grass. He yanked the pistol from Zacarelli's hand and checked for a pulse.

"Flynn!" Witkowski shouted. "Are you okay?" More police cars streamed into the shooting scene, disgorging heavily armed APD officers. When his partner did not respond he told the newly arrived officers to surround the building, focusing on the front entryway, while he went to check on Flynn.

Witkowski found Flynn cowering around the corner of the building. Flynn sat on the ground, trembling, gun in hand. Witkowski carefully took Flynn's pistol and tucked it back into its holster. "Are you hit?"

Flynn shook his head. "He had a gun."

"I believe you, partner. You got him. Can you get back to the car?"

"I think so."

Witkowski helped Flynn to his feet. "Stay there while we clear the building." He trained his gun on the entryway and covered Flynn as his shaken partner made his way toward their patrol car.

Witkowski adjusted his bulletproof vest, then climbed the stairs up to the entryway with a pair of veteran officers, Chuck Nesmith and Emily Young. Guns drawn, the trio charged through the doorway, Witkowski shouting, "Police! Drop your weapons and get on the floor!"

They stood just inside the entryway, their pistols sweeping the area in front of them. Witkowski snapped on his flashlight and scanned the shadows. The beam hovered on a body lying way off to the side near an old confessional.

Witkowski glanced at Nesmith and Young. "Cover me." He crept carefully up to the body and poked it with the toe of his boot. Witkowski jumped back when a noise somewhere between a groan and a grunt spilled from it. As the man rolled onto his back, Witkowski was slammed in the face by the acrid stench of urine and cheap alcohol.

He aimed his pistol. "Don't move!"

The man did not heed Witkowski's order, instead

struggling to a sitting position. He shaded his eyes from the flashlight's bright beam and slurred, "Why you botherin' me, man? I just tryin' to get some sleep." It appeared to Witkowski that this was a squatter with a drinking problem. The drunk had a death grip on a bottle of hooch swaddled in a crumpled paper bag.

"Who are you?" Witkowski demanded.

"Jake," the man said. "Why you in ma house?" He let out a massive belch followed by laughter.

"Get up, old-timer. You don't belong in here," Witkowski said. He turned to Nesmith. "Take this guy outside. Hold him for the ambulance." The homeless guy lurched to his feet. Nesmith snatched the bottle from him and tossed it aside, then performed a quick pat, finding no weapons. The squatter bowed with a flourish, then stumbled to the doorway. He stepped out into the bright sunlight, grabbed the rusty handrail, and wobbled his way down the stairs. Witkowski shook his head in amazement, then proceeded to clear the rest of the building.

The old man didn't seem to notice Zacarelli's dead body as he staggered past it. As they reached the police car, he urinated in his pants. "Sonofabitch," Nesmith said. The old man plopped down, his back against the vehicle. "You stay there and don't move. The ambulance is on its way." He yelled to a recently-arrived police officer to watch the old man, then dashed into the church to help Witkowski clear the rest of the building.

By this time, the area around the vacant church was pure chaos. APD officers were doing their best to keep the growing crowd of spectators from overrunning the scene. In all the confusion, the homeless drunk staggered away unnoticed. Two streets over he ducked behind a thick hedgerow, ditched the old clothes, and Phil Crowley emerged.

Chapter Forty-Eight
USS *Slater* (DE-766)
Albany, NY
July 4, 12:46 PM

I leaned around the edge of the open hatch for a quick peek at what was happening, then immediately pulled back. The flying bridge appeared to be a very small area populated by too many people. I knew even one stray shot was guaranteed to hit somebody.

I closed my eyes trying to fix all the players' positions. Rockwell had his back to me. He stood next to something called a pelorus, according to the diagram affixed to the bulkhead across from the open hatch. It looked like a giant compass on top of a pedestal. Unfortunately, the damn thing was right between Rockwell and me. No clear shot there, and if there was, could I shoot a man in the back, even an armed man? I didn't think so.

A buzzing sound approached and grew louder as I stood inside the hatchway trying to figure out what the hell I was supposed to do. Glancing out the open hatch again, I caught a glimpse of something in the air moving slowly over the bow of the *Slater*, starting over the water and creeping toward the dock. I hoped it was a police helicopter, but I didn't feel that lucky.

It turned out to be a large black drone trailing red, white, and blue streamers and a banner with Clifton's name on it. Right in the middle of a deadly hostage situation involving the governor of New York on the top deck of the warship, some idiot was flying a campaign drone.

Back to business, Patterson. I knew where Rockwell was. Everyone else was lined up in front of him, left to right: Dawson, Kohler, a photographer, Clifton, and a videographer. Clifton was dead-center in front of him, Rockwell aiming his pistol directly at her. The more he screamed, the more the gun wavered. *Where the hell was my backup?*

Lieutenant Dawson was trying to talk Rockwell down from whatever it was he planned to do but the maniac with the gun kept threatening to shoot Dawson if he didn't shut up. Rockwell was getting more agitated. If this went on much longer it would be a bloodbath. I had to make my move now but I had to be careful not to spook him. That might be all it took for the bullets to start flying. I yanked the useless tablet from my forearm and removed my jacket, leaving them both just inside the open hatch. I holstered my weapon and stepped slowly out onto the flying bridge, my hands held high.

"Hey, Rockwell," I said, trying not to sound too loud. He swung around and stared at me wide-eyed. All I could see was his pistol aimed right at my center mass, way too close to miss. The guy looked real jumpy. "Whoa, whoa," I said. "Easy. I'm just here to help you out of this mess."

"Lose the gun," he said. "Slow. Real slow. Thumb

and index finger only." He swept his pistol back and forth between me and the line of people in front of him.

"Gotcha," I said. "You're the boss, okay?" I slid my pistol out using only my right thumb and forefinger, then held it up for him to see. I started to lay it on the wood grating under my feet.

"No," he said.

"No, what?"

"Over the side. And make it a good toss."

"Whatever you want." I took a last look at the new pistol I had just finished paying off. *Some days I just couldn't catch a break*. I tossed it. Two seconds later I heard it hit the water off the starboard side of the ship.

"Close the hatch." Rockwell motioned toward a long block of wood. "Wedge that between the hatch and bulkhead." I made sure to move real slow as I followed his orders. "Now get over here." He used the muzzle of his pistol to indicate he wanted me in line with the others.

"You need to give me that gun right now before this goes too far," Dawson said.

"I told you to shut the hell up!" Rockwell said. "You open your mouth one more time and you're dead!"

We all looked up as the drone made another circuit around the *Slater*. I could have been wrong, but I could swear Rockwell had a smile on his face as he tracked it across the bow of the warship, then checked his wristwatch.

It was time for me to try to thin the herd. Clearing my throat to get Rockwell's attention, I said, "It's kind of crowded up here. Maybe it would be a good idea to let the photographer and videographer go. You can't see any harm in that, plus it makes you look good." Rockwell frowned. "Just saying, man."

"Nobody moves."

I tried again. "Wouldn't it make more sense to let them go down to the main deck and record this whole thing? Once it hits the internet your message will get out to the world." Dawson gave me a look that said, *Don't give this maniac any ideas.*

Rockwell pointed his weapon at the videographer and photographer, then waved them to the hatch. "Go. I want the world to see what happens next." Then he addressed me. "Block that hatch again after they leave. And if anybody comes through there, Clifton will be the first to die."

I moved the block of wood, opened the hatch, and ushered the photographer and videographer through. A knot of APD officers had assembled at the foot of the ladder. One of them motioned to me to be quiet. He began to ascend the ladder followed by more of his fellow officers, but to his surprise I slammed the hatch shut and jammed the block of wood back in place. The lead officer pounded on the hatch but there was no way I was going to let them up here. We were sitting on a powder keg with a real short fuse. More guns would guarantee a quick end for the hostages.

Now there were only five of us on the flying bridge: Dawson, Kohler, Clifton, Rockwell, and me. Rockwell waved for me to stand by Clifton. I did, my back to the warm steel bulkhead overlooking the dock. I chanced a quick glance over my shoulder at the dock below. It was pure chaos. Men and women in various uniforms were trying to get the crowd back behind the barricades but they weren't having much luck. Thousands of arms holding smartphones in the air were pushing closer to the *Slater*, everyone hoping to get that perfect video and post it on the internet for their fifteen minutes of fame.

The drone buzzed by again. I wondered why

Rockwell wasn't pissed off seeing it up there advertising Clifton's campaign. Something wasn't adding up. And again, he glanced at it with a smile like he was happy it was there. And again, he checked his wristwatch.

"You know why I'm doing this, right?" Rockwell growled at Clifton. "You know me."

Clifton had been silent up to this point. "I have no idea who you are."

Rockwell pointed the gun right at Clifton's face.

"Easy," Dawson said.

"I told you to shut up!" Rockwell turned the gun on Dawson.

"Hey!" I shouted, bringing Rockwell's attention back to me. "Easy, man," I said. "Just tell the governor what this is all about."

Rockwell was huffing and puffing like an overworked quarter horse, staring at me long enough to make me think I'd overplayed my hand. He finally spoke to Clifton.

"I'm Gregory Rockwell." Helen Clifton shrugged. "My parents are Suzanne and Thomas Rockwell." Clifton's eyes opened wide, the names well known to her. "They *were* my parents. But you destroyed them because you were so goddamn power hungry." He stepped closer to her, the barrel of the gun inches from her forehead. The drone buzzed past again. And Rockwell smiled again as he watched it sail behind Clifton's head. Somehow that drone was involved in this.

That's when I noticed Andy Kohler wasn't looking so good. His complexion was pasty-white and a heavy sheen of perspiration covered his face.

"Andy, are you okay?" I asked.

Kohler opened his mouth to speak but before he could utter a word, his eyes rolled back into his head and he grasped his chest. He slumped against Dawson, the APD lieutenant guiding him down to the deck of the flying bridge.

"Pills. In my pocket," Kohler gasped. Dawson went through Kohler's pockets, finally pulling out an orange pill bottle. He popped the white plastic top off, shook a pill into his hand, and shoved it into Kohler's mouth. Andy Kohler lay back across Dawson's lap, pinning Dawson to the deck. It was all on me now to stop Rockwell.

Governor Clifton had been quiet until this point. "I had nothing to do with what happened to your parents," she said.

"You had *everything* to do with what happened to them!" Rockwell's face was inches from hers. "You destroyed their lives, everything they worked so hard for, because you *needed* to be governor. They were good, honest people and you destroyed them with your goddamn lies!"

Clifton thrust her chin out defiantly. "It was just politics," she said. "Your father should never have gotten into the game if he wasn't tough enough to play."

Rockwell's eyes just about burst out of his head, his jaw so clenched I thought his teeth would shatter. I had to do something. This guy was about to go off the rails and Clifton goading him on was not helping our situation.

Dawson suddenly shouted, "I think this guy is having a heart attack!"

Rockwell spun on Dawson. "I told you the next time you said something you were gonna die!" He leveled the gun at Dawson's face.

There was no time left. I had to make my move right now.

"Hey!" I yelled as loud as I could. Rockwell snapped

around but left the gun pointed at Dawson. It was now or never. I launched myself away from the steel bulkhead and dove at Rockwell. He brought the gun around but a split second too late as I ducked under it, smashing into his midsection, driving him up against the pelorus with such force he dropped the pistol. Dawson tried to scramble for the gun but he was still pinned under Andy Kohler's slack bulk. Rockwell took a swing at me but was off balance. I leaned back from the near miss, then drove my fist into the side of his head. He went sprawling back, coming to rest against the steel bulkhead. I was pretty sure I had never hit anybody that hard in my life.

I grabbed his gun and tucked it into my waistband, then hauled him to his feet, spun him around, and snapped my handcuffs on him. I turned him back to face me. He had a smile on his face. But he wasn't looking at me. He was looking past me. I grabbed him by the front of his shirt and pinned him against the bulkhead, then glanced over my shoulder. He was staring at the drone. And the sonofabitch was smiling. "What the hell's so funny?"

"I still win," he said. He glared at Clifton and laughed. "I still win! And you're still gonna die!"

I heard the buzz of the drone's motors suddenly kick into overdrive. That's when it hit me—the drone had to be the real weapon. Glancing over my shoulder again, I could see the damn thing diving straight at us.

I pushed Rockwell down, shoved Governor Clifton to the deck, and brought the pistol up. Resting my hands on the edge of the bulkhead, I aimed and emptied the clip.

I hit one of the small motors, throwing the thing off course. It spun drunkenly right over our heads and dropped into the water on the starboard side of the *Slater*.

A second later, a loud explosion sent a huge geyser of water into the air, drenching us all.

Soaked from the water thrown up by the explosion, I stood there with the empty gun in my hand. I could hear the APD officers hammering furiously at the hatch, trying to get it open. Lieutenant Dawson, Andy Kohler, Governor Clifton, and Gregory Rockwell were huddled on the deck around me, all still alive. There was total pandemonium on the dock far below us.

I couldn't help but think back on that night five years ago when I'd failed Dave Taylor in a small alley during a heavy rainstorm that felt oddly like this.

Dawson got to his feet. Without a word, I handed him Rockwell's pistol, then kicked the block of wood away from the hatch. It flew open, releasing a flood of APD officers onto the flying bridge.

I glanced back at Dawson before passing through the hatchway. He smiled and nodded. I took it to mean he thought I'd done a good job. I made my way down to the main deck and walked off the USS *Slater*.

Epilogue
The Caribbean Queen
St. Thomas, U.S. Virgin Islands
April 17, 3:43 PM

The sun sat just above the horizon, bathing the ocean in a yellow so intense that the water appeared covered in molten gold. I leaned on the polished wood railing circling the upper deck of the Caribbean Queen, gazing at the dock far below me. Crew members hustled like an army of ants preparing the large cruise ship to leave the island of St. Thomas. Swarms of passengers rushed along the dock trying to get aboard before they became stranded in paradise. All three thousand-plus passengers had been forewarned that a cruise ship's timetable was carved in stone and nothing short of an apocalypse could change it.

The deck plates vibrated under my feet. The engines were running up. Gangways had been pulled away and mooring lines were being released. With a loud blast from the ship's horn, the Caribbean Queen eased away from the dock amid a roiling of frothy, muddy water stirred up by the huge propellers.

I lingered at the railing watching St. Thomas recede behind us. A long white wake tinged with sparkling gold highlights trailed away from the stern of the ship. This was more peaceful than the last time I was on a ship. I hadn't thought too much about the USS *Slater* until now. Maybe being at sea is what brought it all back.

A lot had happened since I stepped off the *Slater* after defusing the crisis on the flying bridge ten months ago. I was still amazed that no one got killed. Some had called me a hero but I brushed that off. I figured I got lucky, pure and simple. Things could easily have gone terribly wrong for a lot of people that day, me included. Since then, the other players on the top deck of the old warship had gone through some changes of their own, some good, some not so good.

Gregory Rockwell, the man behind the insane plan to kill the governor of New York State was behind bars. The news media said he had suffered the same fate as his father—his mind completely melted down with little hope of ever coming back. Quite a legacy for the poor guy. It's scary to think how close he actually came to accomplishing his mission.

As for his two buddies, Zacarelli was shot and killed by none other than my old nemesis APD Officer Steve Flynn. Sadly, Flynn couldn't get over his first on-the-job kill and was still on modified desk duty for an unspecified period. I ran into Flynn a while after the shooting and, to my surprise, he was cordial. Will wonders never cease.

Crowley, the real brains behind the drone attack that almost put an end to yours truly, got away, but not for long. A couple of months later he was picked up on a routine traffic stop down in Texas, not too far from the Mexican border. Homeland Security was notified and scooped him up right away. It turns out Crowley was building drones for one of the cartels to ferry drugs and who-knows-what-else back and forth across the border. This guy was one bad hombre, but a bad hombre who would be locked away for a very long time.

My new pal, APD Lieutenant Larry Dawson, contacted me about a month after the *Slater* debacle. He said if I ever wanted back in with the Albany Police Department, he'd put in a good word. I thought about it, but decided to wait a while. Because of the way things worked out with the *Slater*, I had more business as a private investigator than I could handle. And not looking for lost pets or cheating spouses this time. I'm talking real cases with paying clientele. I figured I'd do this gig for a bit and see how it went. It's good to have options.

A big reason my private investigation service was going so well had to do with the story Kyle Fitzpatrick wrote about the whole Rockwell-USS *Slater* escapade. He was the right guy to put it all together since he'd been involved from the beginning. Turns out he was a gifted journalist after all. And it didn't hurt any that I came off looking like a superhero. Kyle's story was picked up by pretty much every big news organization in the world. His personal appearances ran the full gamut from early morning news broadcasts to late night talk shows. The job offers poured in but Kyle was taking his time picking the right one. Not bad for his first time at bat.

Andy Kohler's heart attack during the hostage situation on the *Slater* wasn't as bad as we first thought. He took it as a sign that it was time to retire from politics. From his hospital bed, Kohler told Helen Clifton to take the job and stick it. Kohler gave me a big break when I was down and I would be forever in his debt. He was truly one of the good guys.

Helen Clifton didn't fare too well after her

connection to Gregory Rockwell was exposed. No one quite believed she was the poor victim in spite of the guy trying to kill her. Clifton's opponents started digging and the skeletons they uncovered from long ago graves smashed into her presidential campaign like a runaway freight train. Every day brought a new scandal. Eventually her sky-high poll numbers tanked. Soon, her own party faithful distanced themselves. The once-revered Helen Clifton was damaged goods in the political arena. Who knew the public had finally had its fill of dirty politics, instead searching for a kinder, gentler leader? I figure that's a search that won't end anytime soon.

The sound of giggling brought me back to the here and now. A trio of children scurried behind me, their young parents struggling to keep their herd together. The lush island of St. Thomas was almost out of sight. The setting sun kissed the horizon. I gripped the rail with both hands, closed my eyes, and breathed deeply, letting the clean ocean air fill my lungs, the warm tropical breeze wafting over me. It felt good to be alive.

"Hey, you," a soft voice said.

A slim arm wrapped around my waist and I opened my eyes to see Megan Fitzpatrick standing next to me at the railing. Her tanned face glowed in the setting sun, the soft breeze flicking her raven black bangs across her forehead. I stared into her glittering green eyes. If this was a dream I hoped I would never wake up.

"You okay?" Megan tilted her head.

I placed my hands on her shoulders. "Never better."

"Looked like you were a million miles away."

"No, just thinking."

"Yeah?" She pressed up against me. "About what?"

I had been thinking about the afternoon I finally left the *Slater* and caught a taxi to Albany Medical Center where Megan was recovering. I rushed into her room, clothes still dripping wet from the water thrown up by the near-miss explosion. She had stared at the soaking wet idiot in her doorway, but only for a second, then held her arms out. I dropped into those arms that I'd stupidly pushed away years ago and we both let the tears flow. Kyle rose from his chair and excused himself, quietly closing the door behind him.

I couldn't get my apology out fast enough, telling Megan how sorry I was for what happened between us years ago. And what was her reaction? She held my face in her hands, smiled, and said it was all behind us now. Then she kissed me and every bad thing that had happened to me over the years since we'd broken up dissolved.

The nurse on duty was a real sweetheart. She took my wet clothes and gave me a set of scrubs to wear. Megan and I talked for hours. It felt like we'd never been apart. Sounds like a sappy Lifetime movie but this was the real deal, one of those second chances you always prayed for but never got. There was no way I would blow this again.

After Megan was released we began to see each other and the magic was still there. And here we were, ten months later, vacationing in the Caribbean together, just like the good old days.

"Just thinking about how we got here," I said.

"Don't overthink the situation, Patterson." Megan smiled.

All I could do was grin like a fool.

"What's so funny?" she asked.

"Dave Taylor used to say that all the time." I glanced down at my watch, suddenly realizing it was April 17th. "Today is the anniversary of Dave's shooting," I said. "I had forgotten all about it."

"We'll stop and see his wife when we get home," Megan said softly. "For now, let's just walk and enjoy the evening together."

We strolled along the deck, arm in arm, the sky turning indigo above us. Megan wore the brooch I had surprised her with years ago on our last trip to the Caribbean. After using the brooch to escape from Rockwell's prison, she was never without it. If she wasn't wearing it, the brooch was in her pocket or purse. She said it was like her version of a Swiss Army knife, the best piece of jewelry she'd ever received.

Megan snuggled closer as we walked. Her hold on my arm felt more right than anything else in my life ever had. My free hand toyed with another piece of jewelry in my trouser pocket that I'd picked up just before we went on vacation. I wasn't sure if it could ever take the place of her lucky brooch, but if I'd learned anything from the incident on the USS *Slater*, it was that life was full of gambles. I felt pretty confident about this roll of the dice as I slipped an engagement ring from my pocket and dropped to my knee. The sparkle in Megan's emerald eyes and her radiant smile told me I'd come up a winner.

ACKNOWLEDGMENTS

Special thanks to Robyn Ringler, owner of East Line Literary Arts in upstate New York, for her diligent editing and superb suggestions. The editing magic she creates with her ever-present stack of #2 pencils is amazing. Robyn has definitely made me a better author.

Thanks and love to my daughters, Katie and Joanna, for always believing in their dear old dad.

My deepest gratitude to all the readers out there who helped to make my first novel, *The Devil's Claw*, the success it is today. I greatly appreciate your emails and the reviews you take time to leave.

IN MEMORIAM

John N. Pignatelli,

my older brother

Jim Stallworth and Gary Williams,

my college buddies

Enid Walker,

a coworker and friend

Tom 'Tommy G' Griesau,

the brother-in-law of a good friend.

All good people, all gone too soon.

ABOUT THE AUTHOR

Nick Pignatelli was born in Troy, NY and grew up in the neighboring community of Wynantskill. He attended college at the State University of New York at Farmingdale on Long Island, NY where he received a degree in Aerospace Technology.

Nick spent a few years writing advertising copy and restaurant reviews for a newspaper before moving on to a long career in Information Technology with a New York state government agency. He retired in 2010 to concentrate on writing and after two years completed work on his first novel, *The Devil's Claw.*

Nick is a lifelong resident of upstate New York, the setting for both *The Devil's Claw* and *The Politics of Murder*, and currently lives in Clifton Park with his wife, Joyce. In his free time, Nick enjoys traveling, reading, and playing guitar.

Made in the USA
Middletown, DE
16 November 2017